GLADIATOR SCHOOL
BOOK 6

BLOOD JUSTICE

DAN
SCOTT

SCRIBO
A division of Book House

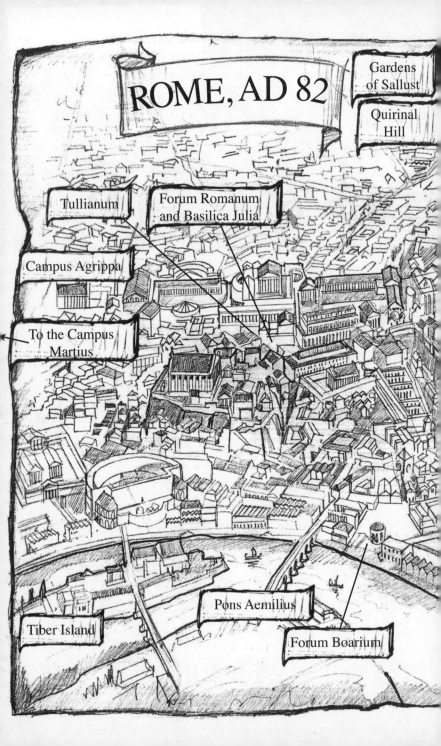

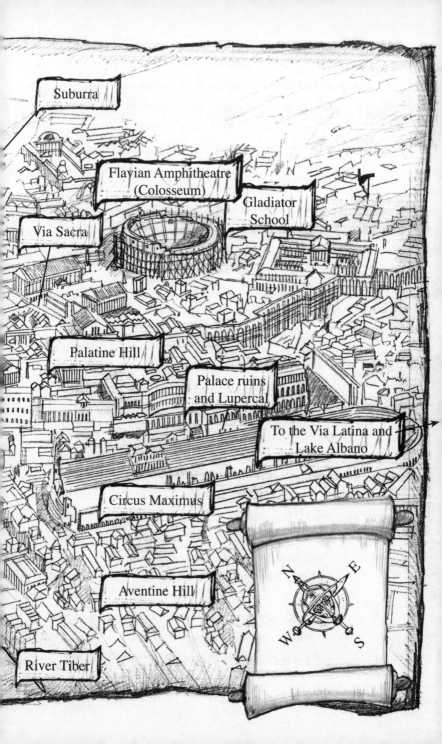

Reader reviews of Gladiator School 1: *Blood Oath*

'I would not put it down.'
GRACE PARKER, AGE 10

*'Scott does a good job of creating the primary characters and
bringing the world of a 1st century gladiator vibrantly to life
for young readers without glamorizing it. . . .
There is enough suspense to propel the story nicely and
instructive material is woven expertly into the narrative . . .
without extended dull or tedious explanatory passages.'*
MARY HARRSCH, ROMAN TIMES

*'[My son and I] especially liked the use of Latin in the book
with the brief footnotes to explain what the words meant. The
story certainly takes some very unexpected turns and gives a
good sense of place and time.'*
DAVID OGILVY

*'A story set in Ancient Rome with many contemporary
echoes. . . .* Blood Oath *gives a vivid picture of ancient Rome
and doesn't shy away from the ferocity of the gladiator arena
or the reality of death . . . The friendship between Lucius and
the Egyptian slave Isidora is well developed and as a reader
I really cared about them.'*
**ROSEMARY HETHERINGTON, INIS, THE CHILDREN'S
BOOKS IRELAND MAGAZINE**

THE MAIN CHARACTERS

Lucius, a Roman teenager

Quintus, his older brother

Valeria, their younger sister

Caecilia, their mother

Isidora, Lucius's friend, a freedwoman
(ex-slave) from Egypt

Faustina, Valeria's friend

Glabrio, Consul of Rome

Gaius, a young lawyer, son of the murdered
senator Canio

Crassus, a lanista (trainer of gladiators)

PROLOGUE

THE SHADOW

ROME
15 JULY AD 82

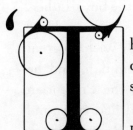here's someone following us, I'm sure of it,' said Lucius, glancing over his shoulder.

'Well then don't look at him,' muttered Quin. 'Keep facing forwards.'
His hand moved to the hilt of his sword, a habitual reflex whenever danger threatened.

'It can't be far now, can it?' asked Isi.

The boys didn't reply, their minds preoccupied with the mysterious shadow to their rear. Lucius was absolutely sure that someone was there. Yet when he risked another peek behind him, he could see no one suspicious among the bustling crowds of pedestrians.

They were back in Rome. Their ship had docked that morning, and they were now walking along the

Alta Semita, a road taking them northeast towards the Quirinal Hill. It was a hot day, and the smells of the city were always at their worst on days like this: smells of sewage, sweat and manure wafted in from the run-down district of Suburra to the south.

On their left was the Campus Agrippa.* The park contained an enormous map of the Roman Empire, engraved on a marble slab. Seeing it reminded Lucius of his recent adventures in far-flung places – Carthage, Ephesus and, most recently, Britannia. He was pleased to be back in Rome, but also scared: this was where Consul Glabrio's power was at its strongest. Glabrio was their mortal enemy. He had killed the boys' father, Aquila, and was now determined to kill them. Here above all he had the means to do so. He wielded great influence over the new emperor, Domitian, and he controlled the emperor's elite troops, the Praetorian Guard. He dominated the Senate and had spies and informers everywhere. Returning to Rome was, in many ways, like entering the lion's den. But Lucius, Quin and Isi felt they had no choice. If they were to defeat Glabrio and avenge the murder of Aquila, they had to do it here.

As well as killing Aquila, Glabrio had also murdered the emperor Titus, Domitian's brother and predecessor. Tucked beneath Lucius's arm and hidden by his cloak was a small leather casket containing two

* *Campus Agrippa: a park and racecourse named after the great statesman and general Marcus Vipsanius Agrippa.*

vital pieces of evidence that would help them prove this. The first was an autopsy report written by Diomedes, Titus's physician, concluding that the emperor had been killed by poison. Glabrio had ordered Diomedes to burn this report and write a new one stating that Titus had died of a fever – but Diomedes had made a copy of the original report. This was that copy. The second document in the chest was a statement signed by Diomedes declaring that the official autopsy report was false and that Glabrio had forced him to rewrite it.

These documents probably weren't enough by themselves to bring down the all-powerful consul. They now had to find someone with sufficient stature, integrity and courage to present the evidence against Glabrio in court. The one man in Rome who possessed all of these qualities, and who would be prepared to stand up to Glabrio, was Senator Aulus Pomponius Licinius. It was to Licinius's residence on the Quirinal Hill that they were now heading.

They passed through the Porta Sanqualis in the Servian Wall, the six-hundred-year-old defensive barrier that surrounded the inner part of the city, and began the steep climb up the hill. They passed temples and ancient, mossy tombs, some of them dating back to the early Sabine settlers on the hill, before the founding of Rome. After cold, wet Britannia, the heat of the Roman summer was hard to tolerate, and very soon their under-tunics were damp with sweat. Before their arrival in Rome, Lucius and Quin had swapped their legionary uniforms for civilian togas, and Isi had replaced hers with a ladylike stola. That way they were less likely to stand out, and the clothing gave them a status that would hopefully allow them access to a man such as Licinius.

Senator Licinius lived on the fashionable north side of the Quirinal, where many of Rome's wealthy patrician class had their homes. The house was an imposing, red-brick structure built into the side of the hill. Lucius was reassured by the size and bulk of the property. Here, he was certain, lived a man who would be able to help them. They therefore felt reasonably confident as they approached the doorway of the house.

Then Isi stopped.

'Cypress branches,' she said.

'What?' said Quin.

She pointed. A dark fear entered Lucius's heart as he took in the sight of the cypress boughs placed above the fine arched entrance.

They were the sign of a house in mourning.

They knocked on the door, and the porter, wearing dark colours and a solemn expression, opened it.

'Is the master at home?' Quin asked.

'The master,' the porter informed them, 'is dead.'

As he heard these words, Lucius felt a heavy weight dragging him down into the earth.

Of course he was dead! What did they expect? Everyone who opposed Glabrio ended up dead!

Aulus Pomponius Licinius, they learned from the porter, had met with an appalling accident only a few days earlier. While out boar-hunting in the Sabine Hills to the northeast of the city, one of his companions had accidentally speared him.

Shock and depression filled all three of them as they dragged themselves away from Licinius's house. Whether it really was an accident, or murder made to seem like one, the end result was the same: Licinius, the only man capable of helping them, was no more. Lucius felt, more than ever before, a sense of powerlessness. Perhaps they were in over their heads. Glabrio had all the forces of the state to draw upon, while he, Quin and Isi had virtually nothing – just two flimsy parchment scrolls. It seemed as though they had reached a dead end. For the first time, he couldn't think of what to do next.

Under a cloud of gloom, they descended the north side of the hill down a winding, tree-lined path, and entered the Gardens of Sallust. This manicured landscape of walkways, sculptures, lawns and flowerbeds, which lay between the Quirinal and Pincian Hills, failed to lift their spirits. They sat on a bench, wiped their sweat-drenched faces and tried to decide on their next move. Quin was all for going to the praetor and presenting the evidence to him. The praetor was the city's senior magistrate. He would have the power to call a trial.

'But he's almost certainly under the thumb of

Glabrio, like every other official in Rome,' pointed out Lucius. 'If we go to the praetor's office, you can bet your life they'll treat *us* as the guilty ones. They'll arrest us and put us on trial for treason.'

'But a trial is exactly what we want!' insisted Quin. 'We can use the opportunity to show the documents in public.'

'They'd never allow it,' said Lucius. 'The documents will be destroyed and we'll be declared guilty and executed before any of the real story is allowed to leak out.'

'Are you saying there isn't a single person in this city whom we can trust?'

'There might be,' said Lucius, 'but we have no way of knowing who it is. I say we lie low for a while – hide out somewhere until we can find someone who can help us.'

'And every day we delay, Glabrio gets stronger…' scowled Quin, thumping his fist against the stone seat of the bench.

Lucius knew how much his brother hated inaction – but what other choice did they have?

'And don't forget,' Quin added, 'he's going to marry Mother soon, and then our family's property will officially pass into his hands. Even if we manage to kill or disgrace him, we'll have a devil of a job trying to wrest what's ours from his heirs and descendants.'

Lucius had to admit that this was a good point. Time was definitely not on their side.

'We could try and scare him,' suggested Isi.

'How?' asked Lucius.

'By going out into the streets at night and painting pictures of Glabrio stabbing Titus in the back with the words "emperor killer" underneath…'

'Now there's an idea!' said Quin, a smile at last dawning on his face.

Isi wasn't finished: 'And we could try using your fame to our advantage, Quin… You saw what happened in Londinium, so far from the scene of your great victories. Imagine what would happen if people around here found out you were still alive! You know how much they love you in this city – particularly the poor. What if we start rumours in the slums of Suburra that the Phoenix of Pompeii is alive and well and is coming to exact revenge on Glabrio? Just imagine the shiver of terror that would give him when he hears about it. He might control the senators and the Praetorians – but, if we play this one right, we could control the mob.'

Quin's eyes lit up at the sound of this. 'By the gods, you're right, Isi! That's exactly what we should do! We should appeal directly to the people of Rome. When we show them the proof of Glabrio's guilt, it could lead to a full-scale riot. Glabrio won't know what hit him.'

'Hold on,' said Lucius. 'Wouldn't all that draw attention to ourselves? He doesn't know we're here yet, and we could use that to our advantage…'

'Shhh!' hissed Quin suddenly.

'What is it?' asked Lucius, looking around.

Quin drew his sword and began moving in a crouched posture towards a statue on the other side of the path. 'Thought I saw someone moving behind there,' he whispered. 'Maybe it's the same one who was shadowing us earlier.'

The white marble statue was known as 'The Dying Gaul'.* It showed the slumped figure of a man with a sword wound in his chest. The man's wild hair and moustache, and the torc** around his neck, reminded Lucius of the natives he'd encountered in Britannia. For a second he thought he saw a dark, blurred movement just behind the Gaul's right shoulder. Quin crept closer, so that he was near the Gaul's knee. Then he suddenly pounced like a cat, diving right over the statue and smothering whoever was lurking behind it. There came a squeal of fright, and Quin rose to his feet, dragging a thin, lanky figure up with him. He had grasped the young man by the neck of his toga, while at the same time pointing the tip of his sword towards his cheek.

'Why are you spying on us?' Quin growled. 'One of Glabrio's men, are you? Planning to sneak off and tell your master where we are?'

'N-n-n-' was all the terrified young man could stutter.

'Speak if you value your life!' roared Quin.

* *The Dying Gaul: a real statue found in the Gardens of Sallust.*
** *torc: a necklace made of strands of metal twisted together.*

'P-p-please,' said the man. 'D-d-don't kill me. I'm a f-f-friend.'

Quin let the sword drop to his side. The young man was unarmed and clearly no threat to them. Yet Quin continued to hold him by the scruff, in case he tried to make a run for it.

'Who are you?' Lucius asked.

The young man cleared his throat and tried to draw himself to his full not-very-impressive height. He was a boy of perhaps Lucius's age, but a good deal shorter and slighter of build. 'I am Gaius Horatius Canio,' he said, 'son of the late Galerius Horatius Canio.'

Senator Canio, as they all knew, was the only witness, besides Aquila, to the murder of Titus.

Lucius stared hard at him, and began to discern faint similarities between the boy standing before them and the senator whom he'd met for the last time in Ephesus three months earlier. The boy had the same round face and earnest expression as his father.

'I apologise for following you,' said the boy. 'But I had to be certain that you were the people I've been searching for. You see, I want the same as you: revenge. And if we act together, I think we can do it. We can destroy Marcus Acilius Glabrio.'

PART ONE

ON TRIAL

CHAPTER I

uin released the young man, Gaius Canio, from his grasp. He eyed him sceptically. 'How did you know who we were?' he asked.

'Claudia, widow of Diomedes, described you to me,' he replied.

'You visited her, too?'

Gaius nodded. 'You're Quintus, yes?' He looked at the other two. 'And you must be Lucius and Isidora. Claudia told me that you'd travelled to Britannia to try to get hold of the autopsy report on Titus. So when I happened to catch sight of you back here in Rome, I knew you must have succeeded in your quest.' He nodded towards the little chest partially concealed beneath Lucius's cloak. 'With the evidence you've got

23

there, and my skills, we can't fail.'

'Your skills?' said Lucius doubtfully.

'I'm a trained lawyer,' said Gaius. 'I plan to file a lawsuit against Glabrio and sue him for the murder of the emperor.'

When Quin heard this, he began to giggle. Before long this turned into a chuckle, and then into a full-blown laugh. Soon he was bent over double, so full of mirth that he could barely stay on his feet. Even Lucius and Isi couldn't stop themselves from smiling.

'I don't see what's so funny,' said Gaius, looking a little piqued.

'You?' chortled Quin, wiping his eyes. 'A trained lawyer? Suing Glabrio? How many cases have you fought so far in your illustrious career, Gaius?'

'Well, none so far, as it happens, but…'

The rest of what he said was drowned out by another wave of laughter from Quin. 'Oh, great!' he guffawed. 'Marvellous! Thank the gods! We're saved. Saved by the trained lawyer who hasn't yet fought a single case. Jupiter be praised! This fifteen-year-old trained lawyer, without a single case to his name, is going to wipe the floor with the most powerful man in Rome.'

'Seventeen, actually,' said Gaius.

'What?'

'I'm small for my age,' he said. 'And, OK, I'm young and inexperienced. But I've learned lots from seeing my father in action over the years. I've been attending civil and criminal cases in the Forum since I was seven years old. I know the customs and language of the law courts as well as anybody. This is the moment I've been waiting for – a chance to put my knowledge to good use by bringing down the tyrant Glabrio.'

Quin had stopped laughing, though tremors of amusement still shook his body. 'Well,' he sighed. 'You've certainly got guts, Gaius – I suppose that's something.'

'Will you come with me to my home?' asked Gaius. 'I have a villa to the southeast of the city, in the Alban Hills. We could discuss the case there.'

'You have your own villa?' asked Lucius.

'I inherited it from my father. I live there alone, apart from the slaves. It's got its own bathhouse.'

Lucius, Quin and Isi drew closer to each other to discuss the offer amongst themselves.

'The lad's clearly mad,' said Quin.

'Maybe so,' said Lucius, 'but it's not as though we have too many other options. He's offering us a villa outside the city where we could lie low for a while.'

'A villa with a bathhouse,' sighed Isi.

It didn't take them long to decide what to do.

'We'd be delighted,' Lucius told Gaius.

'That's fantastic!' The boy looked genuinely overjoyed.

The four of them headed back into the hot, foul-smelling city, walking south through Suburra, past the Flavian Amphitheatre, the Palatine Hill and the

Circus Maximus until they reached the start of the Via Appia.* Lucius and Quin kept their heads bowed and tried to look anonymous. There were few senators about – most had swapped the heat and stink of the city for their villas in the country – but the boys' faces were well known to the units of Praetorians who roamed the streets. As they passed the Palatine, Lucius's thoughts inevitably turned to his sister Valeria, forced to live at the top of that hill with Glabrio, her father's killer. He wondered how she was able to endure the man's presence near her every day.

From an ostler at the Porta Capena,** Gaius hired a driver, a carriage and two horses – the boy didn't seem to be short of money – and they continued the rest of the journey in relative comfort. From the Via Appia, they turned onto the Via Latina, heading southeast through farms and dusty villages, baking beneath the summer heat. Within twelve miles, they had begun to climb the foothills of Albanus Mons.*** Here, the air was freshened by cooler breezes. They passed a blue circular lake, bright with the sails of pleasure boats, and with the summer homes of wealthy Romans clustered around its shores. Gaius said that the lake, called Lake

---

* *Flavian Amphitheatre: a huge arena for gladiatorial games, known today as the Colosseum; Circus Maximus: a stadium for horse and chariot races; Via Appia: the main road from Rome to the south of Italy.*
** *ostler: stable keeper; Porta Capena: a gate in the Servian Wall on the Appian Way, near the Caelian Hill.*
*** *twelve (Roman) miles: 18.25 kilometres; Albanus Mons: the Roman name for the Alban Hills.*

Nemi, was sacred to the goddess Diana and had been sailed by the emperors Caligula and Tiberius, both of whom used to have houses here.

Before long, they reached Gaius's villa, which was on a ridge overlooking another lake called Lake Albano. They approached the villa along a steep, winding driveway lined with narrow cypress trees. The entrance was a grand, six-pillared portico topped by a triangular pediment.

Quin gave a low, admiring whistle when he saw it. 'I'm surprised Glabrio didn't try to steal this place from you and give it to one of his cronies,' said Quin. 'That's usually what he does with the properties of his enemies.'

'I'm sure he'll get round to it eventually,' said Gaius. 'But he's killed and imprisoned so many of his opponents, he's got his hands full with properties at the moment. Besides, I've deliberately cultivated a low profile, so I appear no threat.'

'I sometimes wish we'd cultivated a low profile,' muttered Lucius. After ten months on the run, he missed the luxuries that he'd once taken for granted – like regular bathing, delicious food and access to a decent library.

They were greeted on the steps by the chief steward, Nicander, a dark-haired man of middle age with a long, heavy face and thick lips. Gaius told Nicander his guests' names but not who they were nor why they were visiting. He said they would be staying for a little while, and could he please prepare rooms and refreshments for them.

'Of course, sir,' said Nicander slowly and deliberately. 'I will inform the staff.' Nicander retreated at a sedate pace into the house.

Lucius wasn't entirely sure what he thought about Nicander, and regretted that Gaius had told him their names. 'He can be trusted,' said Gaius, noticing Lucius's doubtful expression. 'He was a loyal servant of my father's for many years. I've known him all my life.'

He led them into the cool marble atrium where they were invited to sit on benches by the impluvium.*
Slaves brought them platters of fruit and jugs of iced water. Lucius felt his body start to relax and unwind as he sat by the pool and watched the light play on the surface. He crushed a mouthful of grapes with his teeth, letting the sweet juice trickle down his parched throat.

At the far end of the room, Gaius muttered a prayer and laid a gift of freshly cut flowers before the Lares**
in the household shrine. Then he kneeled before a wax death mask, which Lucius recognised as that of Gaius's father, and made a libation*** of wine. Lucius wondered if Gaius knew the circumstances of his father's death – the fact that Lucius had inadvertently led Eprius,

---

* atrium: an entrance courtyard, roofed at the sides and open in the middle;
impluvium: a pool in the centre of the atrium.
** Lares: minor gods, usually associated with the home.
*** libation: wine, oil or other liquid poured out as an offering to a god or spirit.

Glabrio's assassin, to Canio's hideout. He thought he should probably tell him – but not yet.

Nicander reappeared a little while later and showed them to their rooms in the guest wing. The rooms were next to each other and each looked out onto one side of a peristyle* surrounding a formal garden of box hedges, evergreen trees and flowerbeds. Lucius lay down on the sleeping couch in his room, leaving the doors open so he could listen to the sound of water splashing in the marble fountain and enjoy the scent of roses and sweet-smelling herbs wafting in from the garden.

After a little while, he heard light footsteps in the peristyle and Isi came bouncing into his room, a huge grin on her face. 'Isn't this wonderful!' she said, seating herself on a corner of his couch. 'I don't think I've ever been on the receiving end of such luxury in my whole life! I'm off to the bathhouse in a minute and I want complete privacy for the next hour, so don't you dare come in!'

'I promise I won't,' smiled Lucius.

'After that, I'm going to surround myself with my ladies, who'll give me the complete beauty treatment – face whitening, eye make-up, hair, perfume, the works. Don't expect to see me before sunset.'

'Isi, what's got into you?' laughed Lucius. 'What happened to Tycho the Gladiator? You used to be just like one of the lads.'

* *peristyle: a covered walkway supported by columns.*

29

She stood up. 'Yeah, well maybe I need a break from all that. I want to rediscover my inner girl. She must still be in there somewhere!'

'Have fun!' said Lucius as she skipped happily away.

In the evening, before dinner, the four of them gathered in the tablinum.* Lucius's body tingled pleasantly after his bath and massage, and the fresh toga he'd been given felt deliciously soft against his skin. Quin also sparkled, appearing happy, relaxed and refreshed. But Isi's transformation was the most dramatic. Her hair was too short to be styled, so she wore a wig of tight curls, braids and tumbling locks. Her brown face had been whitened, with light pink touches added to her cheeks and kohl applied to her eyes. Lucius was impressed. She looked extremely pretty. But she didn't look like Isi, and he hoped she'd soon return to her senses and go back to the tomboy look he knew and loved.

Gaius seemed much too small for his father's chair, like a child playing at being the master of the house – yet he did his best to act and speak authoritatively. He examined the autopsy report and the affidavit** carefully. 'These are better than I could have hoped

* tablinum: office or study.
** affidavit: a statement made on oath.

for,' he said after reading them. 'They're very effective pieces of evidence and I can see them impressing a jury… But they're not quite enough.' He leaned back in his chair. 'These prove that Glabrio suppressed the truth about Titus's death, but not that he killed the emperor.'

'But surely the one implies the other,' said Quin. 'Why would he suppress the truth unless it was to cover up his own guilt?'

'He's clever enough to think of reasons,' said Gaius. 'He could argue he was doing it for the sake of political stability – to ensure a smooth succession for Domitian.'

'But then he's still got to explain why he didn't investigate the murder later,' Lucius pointed out, 'I mean once Domitian was safely installed as the new emperor. Surely the only possible reason why he didn't was because he was the murderer.'

Gaius shook his head regretfully. 'In legal terms, we'd call that "speculation" or "conjecture" – guesswork, basically – and we can't base our case on that.'

'Well then, what about the unexplained deaths of the two witnesses, our father and yours?' said Lucius. 'That's surely got to raise suspicions.'

'In court, they'd call that "circumstantial evidence" – in other words, there are other possible ways of explaining those deaths, so they're not by themselves sufficient to amount to proof.'

Lucius could feel himself starting to get irritated by

Gaius's nitpicking attitude, and he noticed that Quin was, too. 'You lawyers are so logical,' Quin snapped, 'but you ignore things like basic common sense!'

Gaius looked unfazed. 'I'm just trying to demonstrate what we're up against,' he said. 'Don't forget, Glabrio will assemble a formidable legal team to fight this, and they'll use every trick in the book to wriggle their way out of any charge we bring against them. Our case has got to be watertight, and I'm afraid what we have here is far from watertight. Before I can bring the case to court we'll need to find something else – some piece of evidence that directly links Glabrio to the murder.'

'Well, where in Hades* are we going to find anything like that?' asked Quin. 'Our father's dead. Your father's dead. The cook who put the poison in Titus's food is dead. Glabrio's killed every single witness who could pin the blame on him.'

'I suggest we make a trip to Aquae Cutiliae,'** said Gaius.

'Titus's villa,' said Lucius, 'where the murder took place.'

Quin smiled. 'That's the first sensible thing you've said all evening, Gaius Canio,' he declared. 'We can search the place for evidence. When do we leave?'

'The day after tomorrow,' said Gaius.

* *Hades: the underworld; the abode of the dead.*
** *Aquae Cutiliae: a mineral spring to the northeast of Rome, near present-day Cittaducale.*

'What's wrong with tomorrow?' Quin wanted to know.

'I have business to sort out here at the villa and on the farm. I'm meeting with the estate manager and he's taking me on a tour. But I do hope you can find ways to keep yourselves occupied for one more day. We have an extensive library and an exercise room, and we have a boat moored at the jetty if you fancy a little jaunt on the lake…'

The three guests looked at each other. Lucius spoke for all of them when he said: 'I'm sure we can manage another day.'

The following day would remain for a long time in Lucius's memory as one of the happiest of his life – certainly since the death of his father. Maybe it seemed like that because what followed was so awful – or maybe because it simply was a perfect day. The weather was glorious, with the sun shining out of a brilliant blue sky and a mountain breeze taking the edge off the summer heat. They breakfasted on fresh fruit, bread rolls and fish on a terrace overlooking the courtyard garden. Then they headed down to the lake in the company of a friendly and talkative slave by the name of Cassipor, accompanied by his team of musclebound oarsmen.

The boat turned out to be a luxurious pleasure

barge, which Cassipor claimed had once belonged to the emperor Caligula. Lucius, Isi and Quin gazed wide-eyed at the elegant cedarwood vessel with its jewelled prow and purple sails. It sat low in the water and its graceful curves reminded Lucius of an elongated serving platter fit for an emperor's table. The barge had a series of luxurious cabins below decks, and a bathroom with marble and bronze fittings. It even boasted a small glass mosaic floor offering an underwater view of the lake.

As the oarsmen rowed them out onto the blue waters, Cassipor seated his guests on stools near the stern and taught them how to fish. During the course of the morning they caught, between them, a dozen trout, several perch and a tench. While they sat there with their fishing lines trailing through the silken surface of the water, Cassipor pointed out the birdlife along the shoreline – they saw herons and snipes wading in the shallows, mallards and coots nesting among the reeds, and a marsh harrier diving for prey.

Set back from the lake shore and partly hidden by wild holly and hawthorn bushes was the stone entrance to a mile-long drainage tunnel. Cassipor told them it had been built by the Romans about five hundred years ago, during their campaign against the city-state of Veii. The Oracle at Delphi* had

* *The Oracle at Delphi: oracles were places where priests or priestesses were believed to foretell the future. The one at Delphi in Greece was the most famous in the ancient world.*

apparently foretold that the Romans would not defeat Veii until they had learned how to tame Lake Albano, which often flooded in those days, devastating the local countryside. The tunnel was built with the labour of thirty thousand slaves and, sure enough, within a few years of its completion, Veii was conquered.

Quin was the first to tire of the fishing experience, which required a level of patience and sedentary stillness that was ultimately beyond him. In a fit of impromptu playfulness, he threw down his rod, clamped his arms around his brother's waist, lifted him off his stool and hurled him into the lake. For Lucius, this sudden and unexpected immersion in freezing wetness was a shock to the system after feeling so sleepily relaxed in the sunshine. He surfaced, coughing and spluttering and screaming curses at his brother. The barge was low in the water with a convenient timber lip running around its circumference, so it was easy enough to clamber back aboard. Full of amiable vengefulness, he rounded on Quin who had, by this time, inflicted a similar surprise attack on Isi.

There followed a prolonged playfight between the three of them. In the midst of it, Lucius found himself in an aquatic tussle with Isi near the barge. She dunked him underwater and he pulled her down with him. When they resurfaced seconds later, spluttering and laughing, he looked at her with the water trickling down her face and her eyes so bright and alive, and he was suddenly seized by the desire to kiss her. He grabbed her shoulders, pulling her towards him and pressing his lips clumsily against hers. Her stifled gasp echoed in his ears. It was brief and timid, and when it was over, he could barely look at her, but he sensed her surprise – which matched his own. What had come over him? She was becoming very pretty, but he'd known that for some time. He'd noticed it especially last night when she was all dressed up. That hadn't been Isi, though – it had been some Roman version of her, all pale-faced and with carefully coiffed hair. But this was the real Isi before him now – his friend – brown-skinned and lovely.

'What was that for?' she asked.

Embarrassed, Lucius couldn't answer. He tried to make light of it by splashing her and then diving underwater and grabbing her ankles. When they resurfaced, Isi began swimming away from him at a leisurely pace. He easily caught her. She struggled to free herself, but not too energetically. Then she gave up and let herself be embraced. Lucius felt a strange thrill as he held her. It was like nothing he'd ever known. Her skin felt silky-soft, her body warm, despite the chill of the lake. He kissed her again, and this time she kissed him back. Her mouth was warm and welcoming. He could taste the lake on her lips. He closed his eyes and lingered in that dizzy, blissful state, not wanting it to end. But all too quickly, she withdrew from him. She pushed him away, laughing, and swam back towards the barge. By the time he caught up with her, Quin had reappeared, and the moment was over.

In the afternoon they returned to the villa and the boys made straight for the bathhouse to wash off the lake water and relax and doze in the hot steam. When they were done, it was Isi's turn. By the time she emerged, the light was dimming in the sky, and Gaius was there to welcome them with offers of food and iced water. Lucius was seated next to Isi, who was unmade-up and dressed in a simple but elegant stola. Lucius's mouth still retained the sense-memory of their kiss in the lake and his body was still tingling from the experience. Neither of them had mentioned it since, or behaved any differently with each other – and Lucius was relieved about that. It was as if they'd reached some sort of doorway in their relationship and had just taken a peek through it, but neither of them wanted to pass through to the other side – not yet, anyway – just in case it threatened the friendship that was so precious to them.

Lucius could barely remember feeling so tranquil and carefree as he did that evening, watching the sun go down over the lake and dining on the fish they'd caught there. He couldn't have asked for better company. Gaius was a fine host, and Isi and Quin were two of the three people who meant more to him than anyone else alive (his sister Val was the third, of course). But, somewhere in the back of his happy state, a hollow ache still lingered. How could it not? Glabrio had ripped a gaping hole in the fabric of his life – he'd killed Lucius's father, bewitched his mother, kidnapped his sister and was about to steal his family's lands. When Lucius thought of him, Glabrio scarcely seemed like a man, more like an evil god who had cast his shadow over everything. Yet, surprisingly, even this all-enveloping shadow could be pierced by occasional shafts of sunlight – and this day had been one of them. He retired to bed that evening, smiling with memories of the day and looking forward to their journey to Aquae Cutiliae on the morrow.

His good mood lasted until breakfast the following morning, when Isi made her surprise announcement: 'I've decided I won't be joining you boys on your journey,' she said as she dipped salted bread into the yolk of her soft-boiled egg.

'What?' cried Quin.

'Why?' asked Lucius.

They had to wait for her to finish her mouthful.

'I think I'll be more useful in Rome,' she said eventually. 'I want to try and drum up support on the streets, by telling people that the Phoenix of Pompeii is alive and engaged in the fight of his life against the evil Glabrio.'

'But we don't need to do that any more,' said Lucius. 'We're going to sue him in court, remember?'

Isi shook her head. 'Even if you find your evidence at Aquae Cutiliae, which I doubt, you'll still need the backing of the mob in the Forum if you want to overcome those slimy patrician lawyers. And if you don't find anything, you'll need them even more. I'm going to see if I can deliver the mob for you.'

'The Roman mob is a fickle beast,' said Gaius with distaste, 'and to think one can control it smacks, to me, of hubris.* Those "slimy patrician lawyers" you speak of – they can be very adept at turning a crowd with a pleasing phrase. Sometimes they'll even infiltrate the rabble with their own agents to initiate cheers and jeers in the appropriate places. I've seen it happen. Any mob that you assemble may well end up supporting the other side.'

'I disagree,' said Quin. 'Isi's right to give this a try. We'll need every bit of extra support we can get in this battle, and if the ordinary people of Rome have taken me to their hearts, we should use that. Absolutely we should!'

'Where will you stay?' Lucius asked Isi.

'I'm sure Faustina will put me up,' answered Isi. Seeing the anxious look on his face, she took his hand. 'Don't worry, Lu. I'm not known like you boys are. I'll be safe on the streets.'

'Are you sure you can do this?'

'You saw how I managed to raise that little street army in Londinium. I can do the same here, on a much bigger scale. A whisper here. A rumour there. The magic of your brother's name will do its work.'

---

* hubris: the kind of pride that makes people attempt things that are beyond their abilities.

And so it was settled. Isi was provided with a horse and she set off shortly after breakfast.

'Take care, my girl,' Lucius whispered as he watched her ride down the dusty, winding path that led to the Via Latina.

CHAPTER II

17 JULY

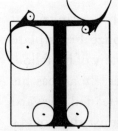wo hours later, Lucius, Gaius and Quin were in the stableyard at the back of the villa waiting for their carriage to be prepared. Nicander was with them, giving orders to the slaves who were packing the rear compartment of the carriage with food, water, blankets and spare clothing for the journey.

In the distance came a sound like thunder. Lucius looked up at the sky, which was the same glorious blue as yesterday, and he wondered how there could be thunder on such a day. The thunder droned on, gradually growing in volume. Suddenly, the air around them crackled with hoofbeats – hundreds of hoofbeats. Before any of them could react, a torrent

41

of glistening metal and quivering horseflesh poured through the gates into the stableyard.

Lucius froze with fear as he took in the white-plumed helmets and the oval shields with their moon-and-stars insignia. This was the Praetorian Guard – the emperor's elite force, now under the control of Glabrio. About fifty of the mounted soldiers entered the yard, quickly and expertly manoeuvring their horses into neat rows, blocking off the gate and any chance of escape. The Praetorians pointed their spears at Lucius and the others in the yard as their horses tossed their heads excitedly, muzzles flecked with foam after the fast gallop up the hill.

One centrally placed horseman broke ranks and trotted a few paces forward. His bronze breastplate seemed to gleam with more lustre than any of his fellow Praetorians, and his crest ran transversely across his helmet, indicating his high rank. He leaned forward in his saddle, resting his forearms against the horse's mane, and peered at Lucius and Quin. 'Quintus Valerius Felix,' he growled. 'Lucius Valerius Aquila. We meet again.'

Lucius looked more closely at the man's craggy face and squinting eyes, and with a flood of recognition he remembered who it was: Tribune Scaro, the man who had captured and very nearly executed them ten months earlier. But how could he possibly have known they were here?

With a horrid, stomach-clenching chill, suspicion

dawned in Lucius that they had been lured into a trap. Gaius hadn't met with his estate manager yesterday – he'd ridden to the Castra Praetoria* outside Rome to tell Scaro where he could find the Valerii boys, no doubt in exchange for a hefty reward – probably immunity for himself from Glabrio's witch-hunt. The whole thing had been a set-up. Gaius had tempted them with his clever lawyerly talk and his offer of the boat and a private bathhouse, and they'd lapped it up like kittens being fed poisoned cream.

In a fury, Lucius turned on Gaius, but his planned tirade died in his throat when he saw the look of genuine shock and horror on the boy's face. It was a relief, of sorts, to know that Gaius Canio, at least, was genuine. But if not Gaius, then who had betrayed them?

'This is private land!' Gaius shouted at Scaro. 'You have no right to be here! These are my guests. Now please leave!' His high voice scarcely carried, though, and Scaro ignored him.

'Where's the third one?' the tribune demanded. 'I heard there was a girl.'

No one answered.

Lucius eyed Nicander, who was currently staring at his sandals and sweating, looking every inch the culprit. He'd had his suspicions about Nicander from the beginning, and perhaps he'd been right. Gaius caught Lucius's stare and turned on the chief steward.

* *Castra Praetoria: the barracks of the Praetorian Guard.*

'Was it you?' he gasped. 'Tell me it wasn't, Nicander. Not you of all people.'

Nicander fell to his knees, an appalled look on his face. 'Master, how can you even think it? I have always been loyal to your family…'

Scaro turned to a person in a hooded cloak riding pillion on a horse a little way behind his. 'You said there was a girl also,' he said. 'An Egyptian. Well, where is she?'

'I–I don't know,' stammered the cloaked figure. 'She was with them when I left here yesterday afternoon.'

Lucius immediately knew the voice, having listened to it for most of the previous morning: Cassipor, the learned, friendly slave who had taught them how to fish and told them the history of the lake. Lucius had never imagined him as a traitor.

Scaro turned his steely gaze on Lucius and Quin. 'On the orders of Marcus Acilius Glabrio, consul of Rome, I'm placing you under arrest. But before I take you away, I demand that you hand over the treasonous document which I know you have in your possession.'

'What document would that be?' Quin enquired innocently.

Scaro glared at him. 'You know very well what document: the fake report by that charlatan Diomedes, making the seditious claim that the divine Titus was murdered.'

'I've never heard of it,' smirked Quin. '*Was* he murdered, then? Is that what they're saying?'

Lucius wished his brother wouldn't goad Scaro, who looked about ready to commit murder himself. Lucius flinched, but wasn't that surprised, when the tribune suddenly let fly with the flat of his sword against Quin's face. Quin fell back against the carriage, clutching his jaw. When he removed his hand, blood was pouring from his mouth, but the defiant twinkle hadn't left his eyes.

'Where is the document?' Scaro asked Lucius.

Lucius shrugged, trying his best to remain calm. 'I don't know anything about any document.'

'Guards, seize them!' roared Scaro.

It was pointless resisting, and Lucius and Quin let themselves be manhandled towards a cage-like wagon with iron bars, standing just inside the gates. On Scaro's orders, heavy iron manacles were locked around their wrists and ankles. After the Valerii boys had slipped through his fingers ten months ago, Scaro was clearly taking no chances. The manacles chafed painfully against Lucius's skin and weighed him down. He was forced into a crouched shuffle as soldiers pushed and prodded them towards the caged wagon. A small gate set within the iron latticework was opened and he was shoved violently onto a floor of sun-bleached wooden planking. A few seconds later, Quin was sent sprawling into the wagon beside him. As they lay there, trying to acclimatise to this new and bitter reality, they heard Scaro bark the same question to Gaius: 'Where is the document?'

Gaius replied that he didn't know what the tribune was talking about, and demanded that he release his guests and get off his land at once. The words were defiant, but his voice had the pitch of a child's, and Lucius wondered what chance they'd have had in court anyway, being represented by someone who sounded so immature.

Scaro bellowed orders to his men to search the villa. Lucius hoped Gaius had had the sense to hide the documents well. He sat up in the wagon and tried to catch Gaius's eye, but the boy was too busy protesting at this 'infringement of his rights as a Roman citizen'. Gaius chased after the soldiers, shaking his fist at them as they tramped into the villa to begin their search. That was the last Lucius saw of their host, before the driver of their prison-wagon wheeled the horses around and started back down the driveway.

A few hours later, Lucius and Quin were back in Rome, languishing in a dungeon cell in the Tullianum, the city's main prison. The Tullianum was in the northwestern corner of the Forum, at the foot of the Capitoline Hill. Almost seven hundred years old according to tradition, it was a dark, dismal place with low, arched ceilings and walls made up of huge, black, ancient stone blocks. The brothers sat next to each other, still in their chains, beneath a fitfully burning oil lamp. Lucius tried to ignore the squirmings in the shadows and the rustles and squeaks of rodents. He blocked his mind to the reek of damp and urine and other putrid smells. Most of all he tried to ignore the sour smell of dread that pervaded the place – for this was the final waiting room of the damned, where generations of convicted prisoners had been forced to live out their final hours before execution.

'Well, here we are again, bro,' said Quin with surprising chirpiness. 'In trouble as usual. Funny how life goes. This time yesterday, I was on top of the world...'

Lucius remembered swimming in the lake, that kiss with Isi...

'Still, we'll get out of this, you'll see,' vowed Quin.

'I wonder if we'll even get a trial,' said Lucius. 'Or will they just execute us?'

'We'll definitely get a trial,' said Quin. 'If they wanted to kill us they'd have done so at Gaius's villa... Surprising in a way that they didn't. I mean, Glabrio doesn't usually hesitate to kill his enemies. You have to ask yourself why he's playing by the rules this time. I reckon it's because he's come under pressure from someone. Maybe the emperor's unhappy with all the blood he's been spilling.'

'Or else Glabrio's just keeping us alive so he can force us to tell him where the autopsy report is,' said Lucius with a frown. 'We may have to be prepared for torture, Quin.'

'Doesn't frighten me,' said Quin.

Lucius sighed. He wished he could be as brave as his brother. He was glad, at least, that Isi would be spared. 'The only good part of all this is that Isi escaped before the soldiers arrived, and she's still free…'

'To cause mayhem on the streets,' chuckled Quin. 'Yeah, she could be our secret weapon – our dux.'*

They heard footsteps coming down the narrow spiral staircase just outside the cell. This was followed by the whining screech of a key being turned in a rusty old lock. The heavy cell door squeaked open and pallid daylight filtered into the dungeon, quickly blocked by the silhouette of a hulking guard.

'Follow me!' he grunted.

They rose with difficulty to their feet and shuffled after the guard. The iron shackles rubbed at the already tender skin on Lucius's wrists and ankles as he and Quin followed the guard up the narrow, twisting staircase.

A few minutes later they were blinking in the bright sunlight of the Forum. Here, they were handed over to six armed guards. One of the guards removed the boys' shackles, much to their relief, and they were then pushed and shoved along at high speed to the Basilica Julia on the south side of the Forum. The nave of this building, which served as a lawcourt and public meeting hall, was breathtakingly huge, with

* *dux: a piece in the Roman board game latrunculi, which had special powers. This is equivalent to the modern expression 'the joker in the pack'.*

endless walls and floors of gleaming marble, and a distant ceiling held up by two lines of crimson-veined marble columns. Sunlight poured down from windows high above their heads. Lucius spotted Gaius near the entrance, pacing nervously. He looked smart in his adult toga, yet tiny in the monumental surroundings. And somehow the toga's voluminous envelopment of his small frame made him seem even smaller.

In this boy lies all our hopes of salvation! thought Lucius gloomily.

When Gaius saw Lucius and Quin, he uttered an excited cry and rushed over to them. A guard tried to bar his way but he shouldered his way past, saying: 'I'm their lawyer, by Jove. Let me through!' His voice sounded shrill and echoey in the vast hall. He grasped them both by the arms. 'Lucius! Quin! Are you all right? I'm so sorry about this. I never thought that Cassipor of all people would prove such a snake.'

'Don't worry,' said Quin, 'it's not your fault.' He dropped his voice to a whisper. 'Did they find anything at the villa?'

'No,' Gaius whispered back. He glanced nervously towards a grand podium at the far end of the nave beneath which a number of important-looking people were chatting in groups. They were all out of earshot, and the guards didn't appear to be listening. 'The soldiers were there for hours,' he said. 'Turned the place upside down, but I hid the papers well.' He smiled enigmatically. 'I suppose that snake Cassipor told you how the Romans defeated the city of Veii.'

The drainage tunnel by the lake!

'But wouldn't Cassipor have thought of that?' hissed Lucius.

Gaius shook his head. 'Luckily, he didn't.'

'Let's just hope the lake doesn't flood,' muttered Quin.

'What's going to happen to us now?' asked Lucius.

'This is a preliminary hearing, held before the praetor,' said Gaius in his normal speaking voice. 'It's where they lay out the charges against you. Then a judge will be appointed and a date set for the trial.'

'What charges?' asked Lucius. 'What are we supposed to have done?'

'I have no idea,' said Gaius. 'Something trumped up, no doubt. It'll be up to me to prove the allegations false. You're the victims here, remember, and this trial will be our chance to put our case. It's not quite what I'd hoped for. I mean...' He broke off and glanced once more at the people gathered by the podium. In a quieter voice, Gaius continued: 'As you know, I'd hoped to gather one more piece of evidence before we went to trial, but it wasn't to be. We'll just have to try and make do with what we've got.'

'What are our chances, do you think?' asked Lucius.

But before Gaius could answer, an official appeared and summoned them to the podium.

As they walked down the long nave, still surrounded by armed guards, Gaius pointed out the key people whom they needed to be aware of. 'The grey-haired, friendly-looking old fellow sitting up there on the podium is the praetor,' he said. 'And see that impressive-looking man on the right?' Gaius pointed to a tall man dressed in senatorial robes, murmuring to a group of his colleagues. 'That's Quintilius Hostilius Sejanus. He's Rome's top advocate, representing Glabrio. He'll be doing his best to prove you two guilty of whatever you're supposed to have done.'

Sejanus had a small, tight mouth set in a large, ruddy face. He watched them approach with a predatory kind of stillness, reminding Lucius of the stare of an ageing leopard he'd once looked after during his time as a beast-handler at the Morning School.

Once Lucius and Quin were standing before the podium, the praetor called for the defendants to be identified. Sejanus adopted a sour expression and pursed his lips as if about to spit out something noxious he'd accidentally eaten. Addressing the praetor, he said: 'Your honour, these are the dangerous young fugitives Quintus Valerius Felix and Lucius Valerius Aquila. These evil brothers have finally been apprehended after many months of searching.'

The praetor leaned forward, peering curiously at Quin. 'I thought Quintus Felix was dead.'

'He is most certainly alive, your honour. As you can see.'

'But there was a funeral…'

'Indeed. And I will go into how that came about

when I lay out the charges against them.'

'Is it generally known that this young man is alive?'

Sejanus leaned closer to the praetor and spoke in a low voice that Lucius strained to catch. 'No, your honour,' he murmured, 'and my client, who is filing the suit against them, would prefer to keep it that way, as such knowledge could lead to trouble on the streets. I hope you understand.'

'Who is your client?'

'Consul Marcus Acilius Glabrio.'

'I see,' said the praetor, his face paling slightly. 'And what are the charges?'

Lucius stiffened, waiting to hear exactly what Glabrio had decided to accuse them of.

'Their list of crimes is long and heinous, your honour,' said Sejanus. 'They range from fraud to mutilation and murder. I will deal with the charges of fraud first of all. During the brothers' first escape from custody ten months ago, they rendered unconscious and then impersonated some priests at the Temple of Cybele on the Palatine. Then, seven months later, the younger brother, Lucius, sedated and impersonated a priest at the Temple of Venus Genetrix, just a short walk from here.'

'Maybe they just really want to be priests,' chuckled the praetor.

Sejanus frowned at this attempt at frivolity. 'It gets worse, your honour,' he said. 'Much worse... A few weeks after that, the brothers resurfaced in

Caledonia* in the company of an Egyptian freedwoman by the name of Isidora, and the three of them used false names and references in order to get themselves recruited as legionaries at a fort over there. The trio were captured shortly afterwards by Caledonian savages. Lucius and Quintus managed to escape and return to the fort, but then showed their true traitorous colours by refusing to reveal the whereabouts of the barbarians' stronghold.'

'My, what adventures they have had!' exclaimed the praetor. 'But what about the mutilation and murder?'

'I will come to that shortly, your honour,' said Sejanus. He cleared his throat. 'When their cover as legionaries was blown, the brothers escaped south from Caledonia to a small town called Aquae Sulis,** where they were apprehended by the military tribune attached to the Caledonian camp, Appius Mallius Lurco. They immediately attacked Lurco and chopped off his hand, before fleeing to Londinium. Lurco, who fortunately survived the assault, would have caught them there, but then a small riot erupted near the amphitheatre and the fugitives escaped under the cover of a mob. We finally managed to track them down this morning at a villa in the Alban Hills.'

Lucius swelled up with outrage at this twisted version of the story.

'Lies!' he heard Quin scream beside him.

* *Caledonia: Scotland.*
** *Aquae Sulis: Bath, England.*

'Speak to General Agricola, if you want the truth!' Lucius shouted, before crying out in pain as a sword butt jabbed him hard in the ribs.

'Keep your mouth shut unless you're asked a question!' a guard's voice grated in his ear.

'Very well, that deals with the mutilation,' said the praetor, ignoring the interruption. 'So what about the murder?'

Sejanus looked grave. 'Now, your honour, we come to the most odious of all the boys' crimes, and the whole reason why they went on the run in the first place.' The lawyer paused dramatically. 'I want to take you back to that sad time ten months ago, just after the death of our beloved emperor, the divine Titus...'

'I remember it well,' muttered the praetor.

'On the night after Titus passed away, with the whole city still in mourning, these boys deliberately and cold-bloodedly murdered their father.'

Spikes, like shards of broken glass, pierced Lucius when he heard this. Shockwaves coursed through him. What perversion of the truth was this? Could Glabrio really be blaming the murder he had committed on the sons of the victim? It felt like the ultimate degradation. He heard Quin shouting, and he joined in. 'How dare you! You monster!' and more in this vein. He felt Gaius's hand on his shoulder trying to restrain him, but he shook him off. 'Liars, all of you!' Lucius yelled.

'*Glabrio* killed our father! Now he's trying to pin the blame on us!'

There was a loud crack and multiple rainbows of pain blazed through his temple. He fell to his knees, clutching the side of his head.

'I told you to keep your mouth shut!' came the guard's voice.

Waves of pain rebounded through Lucius's head. Then he passed out.

CHAPTER III

18 JULY

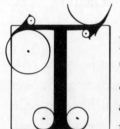he following morning, Lucius and Quin were led back into the Basilica Julia for their trial. Lucius felt groggy and uncomfortable after a night in the rat-infested Tullianum, and his head still throbbed from the blow he'd received the day before. The scene in the nave was rather different today, with many more people present. The praetor was on the podium, as before, seated on a curule chair,* and beneath him and to one side sat a row of distinguished-looking men on a cushioned wooden bench.

Gaius approached them, this time accompanied

---

* curule chair: a chair or stool with crossed legs, used as a sign of office by certain high-ranking officials.

by a couple of assistants, one of whom held the small leather chest containing Diomedes's papers. Lucius was alarmed to see this displayed so publicly, but Gaius reassured him: 'Don't worry, they can't do anything to us now – not even Glabrio. This is a court of law and there are rules. Besides, if Glabrio tried to steal this evidence from us, those men over there would know for sure that he has something to hide.' He pointed to the row of seated men. 'They're the members of the jury – all of them senators,' Gaius explained. 'It's my job to persuade them that you two are innocent.'

'Good luck!' said Lucius, checking out the jurors. They all seemed to be stern-faced men of mature years, unlikely to be persuaded by any argument put to them by a callow youth such as Gaius.

'I was surprised that they decided to hold the trial so soon,' said Gaius. 'I suspect they want to get it over with quickly and without fuss, so we'll have to fight hard to ensure you get a fair hearing. I'm glad, at least, that the praetor has agreed to judge the case. He seems a friendly, well-meaning type.'

Lucius didn't think the praetor looked so friendly today. He wondered if Sejanus or Glabrio had bribed or threatened him last night.

A further set of benches had been placed on the marble steps that rose up on either side of the nave, creating two tiers of seats facing each other. Lucius desperately scanned the faces of the people sitting on these benches for a sight of his sister Valeria, but she wasn't there. His mother was, though – seated very close to Glabrio in the front row on the right-hand side. The sight of the two of them sitting virtually arm-in-arm made Lucius feel sick. He felt Quin stiffen beside him. Glabrio didn't turn to look at them, but remained facing front. His motionless, skull-like head and hooded eyelids reminded Lucius of something cold-blooded and infinitely patient, like a lizard. Caecilia did, however, look towards them. Lucius searched his mother's face for signs of love or affection, or at least support, but found only an expression of deep regret. Her downturned mouth and furrowed brow and the way she inclined her head to one side seemed to be saying: *Where did I go wrong? What did I do to make you turn out this way?* Lucius lowered his eyes, unable to look at this pretence of contrition a moment longer. She seemed so utterly distant to him now. Even if they won the fight against Glabrio, he doubted he would ever be able to think of her as his mother again.

Lucius and Quin were led towards a small square enclosure surrounded by a wooden barricade to the right of the praetor's podium. A gate in the barricade was opened, the defendants were ushered in and the gate was bolted shut. Four heavily armed guards stood sentry around them, a tribute perhaps to Quin's legendary fighting skills. Gaius remained near them, a hand resting on the barricade rail. While an official made some announcements, he leaned towards Lucius and Quin and whispered: 'After you two were taken away, Sejanus finished his list of your alleged crimes. Just wanted to warn you, you're also being charged with killing a young man called Ennius while he was escorting you to Glabrio's house.'

'That's not true!' hissed Lucius. He gritted his teeth. They would fight every single one of these ludicrous accusations. The prosecution had no evidence anyway, so who would believe them?

Sejanus opened the proceedings by setting out the case for the prosecution. Addressing the jury this time, not the praetor, he said: 'I come to you today, esteemed members of the jury, with a case that will make your stomachs churn and your hearts break. A case of fraud, treachery, despicable greed and cold-blooded patricide. These boys standing before you may look young and unworldly, but do not let appearances fool you. Evil, as we all know, can lurk within the most innocent-seeming heart. I intend to prove to you, with the help of multiple eyewitnesses, that Lucius and Quintus, greedy for their inheritance, murdered their father, hoping the incident would be mistaken for the work of an outside assassin.'

As he spoke, Sejanus employed dramatic gestures almost like an actor on a stage. When the jurors gasped in shock upon hearing of the boys' outrageous crime, he raised a hand for silence, as if to say: *Wait a moment… You haven't heard the worst of it yet!* Then he went on to list their other alleged offences, from the cold-blooded slaying of the messenger, Ennius, to the equally brutal amputation of Lurco's hand. He described each crime with all the gusto and enthusiasm of an actor, emphasising the goriness and the cruelty involved. Although Lucius was appalled by the lies Sejanus was spouting, he couldn't help being impressed by the performance, and he began to appreciate why the man was such a successful lawyer. The whole thing seemed unreal, though – almost dreamlike – as if it were happening to someone else. There wasn't a shred of evidence for any of the things he was saying. However good a performer Sejanus was, his case would surely collapse as soon as it was challenged.

Gaius spoke next, putting forward the case for the defence. He told the jurors that his clients were innocent victims of a major conspiracy that involved one of the most powerful people in this city. 'Lucius and Quintus did *not* kill their father or Ennius,' Gaius told the court, 'and if they impersonated some priests and legionaries, and wounded a military tribune, it was only in self-defence – for *they* are the victims here. And it is because they know the identity of the *real* criminal in this case that their lives are now in danger.'

Young Gaius spoke well enough, but unfortunately for him, his voice was too high and wavering to be heard clearly, and although he did his best to pause in the right places and make dramatic gestures with his hands, he lacked the oratorical flair of Sejanus. Also, his mention of a conspiracy involving a powerful person in the city caused such a storm of muttering among the jurors and spectators that he found it even harder to make himself heard.

'I have documents,' he shouted into the noise, 'that will show that Consul Marcus Acilius Glabrio, the man who brought this case to court, is in fact the one who should be in the dock, not my clients. He killed my clients' father to cover up a still greater crime, the murder of Emperor Titus...'

Few heard any of this, and those who did began to boo and hiss the speaker, and even stamp their feet, adding to the din, until the praetor was forced to bang his hammer and call for silence. Lucius surveyed the people howling and jeering from the spectators' benches and realised with a sinking heart that Glabrio must have filled the court with his supporters. When order was finally restored, the praetor asked Gaius if he had finished. Gaius, looking a bit bruised and stunned, said that he had.

With a smug smile, Sejanus leapt up from his seat. 'I would like to call my first witness,' he said. 'Glaukos is a physician who plies his trade at the Circus Maximus, stitching up wounded charioteers. Glaukos, please step forward.'

Lucius could barely believe his eyes as the surgeon of Quin's chariot team, the Whites, came before the podium. Glaukos had been a friend of Quin's. Why was he now testifying against him?

'Glaukos,' said Sejanus. 'On the Ides of September[*]

[*] *Ides of September: the 13th of September.*

62

last year, you were at work in the infirmary of the Circus Maximus, yes?'

'Yes, sir,' mumbled the elderly surgeon.

'Please speak more clearly, Glaukos, so that everyone can hear you.'

'Yes, sir,' said Glaukos in a louder voice. He looked nervous, ill at ease. He kept his eyes on Sejanus, avoiding all eye contact with the defendants.

'Good!' said Sejanus. 'And what were you doing there that morning?'

'I was treating young Quintus after an accident he'd suffered during a race.'

'Was anyone else present?'

'His brother Lucius was there. And later on his father came in, and Senator Canio.'

'Could you describe for the court the nature of the conversation between Quintus and his father?'

'They had an argument. His father didn't want Quintus to race chariots. Quintus did.'

'And how did his father think he could stop a determined young man like Quintus from doing exactly as he pleased?'

'He threatened to cut off his allowance.'

'He threatened to cut off his allowance,' repeated Sejanus, slowly and clearly. 'And how did Quintus react to this?'

'He was shocked, sir. He didn't think he'd be able to live on a charioteer's income.'

'Thank you, Glaukos. I have no further questions.'

The praetor asked Gaius if he had any questions for the witness. Gaius hesitated, then said he didn't. He looked disconcerted by Glaukos's testimony, having known nothing of the argument between Quin and his father, which seemed to provide substance to the prosecution's claim that the boys had murdered Aquila to get his money.

Next up on the witness stand was Mikon, a slave from their household who had been serving at dinner on the night of Aquila's murder. Under questioning from Sejanus, Mikon recalled that his father had ordered Quintus to embark on a senatorial career and, in response, Quin had angrily hurled down his drinking vessel. Lucius had not known him well, but still he was disappointed that one of their former slaves would reveal details of a private conversation between members of a family he had worked for. He wondered what Glabrio had offered him. A great deal, he guessed, because Mikon then proceeded to make a lot of things up. He said that Quin had later become drunk and had begun demanding that his father increase his allowance. Hearing these lies, Quin gripped the handrail of their enclosure until his fists turned white, but managed to maintain his silence.

Suddenly, Lucius had an idea. He leaned across to Gaius and whispered something in his ear. Gaius's eyes lit up at these words, and he whispered an instruction to one of his assistants, who promptly departed, his sandals making echoing clicks upon the endless marble floor of the basilica.

Meanwhile, more witnesses followed. These were gladiators from the Ludus Romanus who recalled conversations with Quin during the days of Aquila's exile, when he'd told them how happy he was that his father was no longer in his life, and had even gone so far as to drop his nomen* Valerius, styling himself simply Quintus Felix. All of the testimony seemed to corroborate the same simple fact: that Quin had hated his father and wanted him dead, so that he could inherit his wealth. Lucius was burning up inside at the lies and distortions being given out on the witness stand. He couldn't imagine how unbearable all this was for Quin. His brother was breathing hard now, nostrils flared, face pale with fury. Of course Quin had occasionally clashed with his father, and it was true that he'd believed the lies being told about Aquila during his exile. But as soon as proof of his father's innocence had been presented to him, he'd shown real remorse and tried his best to atone for his mistake. Lucius knew there had been a deep and abiding love between Quin and Aquila – it was a pity there were no witnesses to testify to that!

Having established a motive, Sejanus then moved on to the murder itself and he talked about how Quin had committed it. He showed, by means of a diagram, how close Quin's room was to his father's and how easily he could have sneaked in during the night.

* nomen: family name.

The most shocking moment of the morning came during the testimony of Vedrix, Aquila's personal valet. Under cross-examination from Sejanus, he explained that his master was having trouble sleeping that night and had asked Vedrix to sleep on a mattress in the corner of the room in case he was needed. Vedrix then said that he saw Quintus come into the room in the early hours of the morning and stab his father through the chest.

This caused howls of outrage from the court. Quin, no longer able to keep a lock on his tongue, screamed at Vedrix: 'How much did they pay you to tell these lies, you worm?'

Lucius was shocked – he'd always trusted Vedrix, and so had Aquila.

More witnesses were called – clients and freedmen* of Aquila's who had been at the house on the morning after the murder. All of them spoke of how calm and decisive Quin had been during that period, ordering a guard on the doors and windows, confining the slaves to their quarters, summoning the city prefect. The impression given was that these were not the actions of a shocked and grieving son, but the efficient behaviour of someone who had planned all this in advance.

Quin shook his head in disbelief, obviously bewildered at how his state of mind that morning had

---

* clients: hangers-on – people who receive, or hope to receive, favours from an important person; freedmen: former slaves who have been set free as a reward for good service.

been misinterpreted.

Lucius looked around for Gaius's assistant. He should have been back by now, with someone in tow who could help them turn the argument around.

'*But what about the brother, Lucius?* I hear you ask,' Sejanus continued when the last of the clients and freedmen had departed the stand. 'So far this has all been about Quintus. So why do we see Lucius standing next to him as co-author of this foul and unnatural deed? To answer that, we must look at what happened subsequently… During the course of the morning, the boys' mother, who had been visiting her dear friend, Consul Marcus Acilius Glabrio, summoned her children to her. She had heard what had happened and was anxious for their safety. So, Quintus, Lucius and their sister Valeria set out for the consul's house on the Palatine Hill, escorted by a slave of Glabrio's called Ennius. On the way there, the boys must have become seized with panic. Worried that their appalling crime was about to be uncovered, they killed Ennius, before fleeing the city.'

'Lies!' Quin shouted. 'All lies!' He pointed his finger at Glabrio. '*You* did it! You, Glabrio, killed Ennius, just like you killed my father!'

'Silence!' shouted the praetor, glaring at Quin.

Glabrio stared back at Quin, the ghost of a smile playing on his thin lips.

'You will not speak, young man, unless or until you're spoken to,' ranted the praetor. 'If you say one more word I'll add contempt of court to the list of charges against you!'

Quin slumped against the rear of their enclosure, looking bewildered, like a wounded bear. Lucius felt for him. This was not his natural arena. He was a man of action, far more at home jousting with a sword than with words.

The praetor adjourned the court for lunch. In the afternoon, a fresh batch of witnesses were called, and this time none of them were people that Lucius or Quin recognised. They included shopkeepers, stallholders, priests and ordinary citizens, and they all said the same thing: that they had seen Lucius kill Ennius in broad daylight on the Via Sacra.* He'd drawn his sword and run him through. The sister, Valeria – so they all said – had screamed and tried to run away, but Lucius had grabbed hold of her and he and Quin had physically dragged her with them.

As these lies rained down on him, Lucius began to feel dizzy. His barely digested lunch began to rise like acid in his throat, and he was sure he was going to faint. The walls and the pillars of the nave started to lose their solidity. They wobbled as if made of aspic. He couldn't believe what he was hearing. So this was Roman justice in action! It may have had the trappings of a courtroom, set in a magnificent basilica with all these fine, distinguished-looking senators sitting in

---

* *Via Sacra: the Sacred Way, the main street of ancient Rome. It led from the Capitoline Hill to the Flavian Amphitheatre.*

judgement, but when it came down to it, there was no justice happening here – not when those with enough wealth and influence could simply bribe witnesses to say anything they chose. This wasn't a trial: it was a spectacle paid for by Glabrio, as grand in its way as a gladiator fight in the Flavian Amphitheatre, but this time with only one possible outcome: the conviction and execution of the accused.

Lucius finally understood what Glabrio was doing, and why he needed to go through the motions of a courtroom trial. He wanted to prove to the world that the Phoenix of Pompeii and his brother were nothing but a pair of murderers. He knew if he'd simply killed them as he'd killed all his other enemies, it could have stirred a popular revolt. By doing things this way, he hoped to nip any such revolt in the bud.

The strategy looked as though it was working. Even if the jurors had been fair-minded men, uninfluenced by Glabrio's money or threats (which Lucius doubted), they would surely have been convinced of his and Quin's guilt by the evidence they had been shown today. Nothing could be done. It seemed that their fate was sealed. Soon, Gaius would get his chance to speak. But what evidence did he have to counter all these many witness statements? A couple of documents? His case now seemed very flimsy indeed.

But then the doors at the far end of the nave opened and Gaius's assistant returned, with a bigger man in tow. Lucius's heart gave a lurch of excitement as he recognised the new arrival. This was the very man he'd been hoping to see – the one whose testimony might just swing things in their favour.

Now it was Gaius's turn to call witnesses. And the first and only witness he called to the stand was the man who'd just arrived. 'Pavo,' Gaius said to him. 'You worked as a guard at the house of the Valerii on the Esquiline Hill, is that right?'

'Yes, sir,' said Pavo.

Lucius remembered Pavo coming to them on that terrible morning ten months ago – the morning of his father's death. Pavo had told them of his tussle with an intruder the previous night. He'd been standing guard in the portico at the front of the house when he saw a hooded figure clambering down a pillar from the roof. He'd grabbed him, ripping the fellow's tunic, revealing a tattoo of a kestrel with an arrow through its heart. The intruder – who Lucius later found out was his so-called friend Eprius – then clouted the guard and escaped. If Pavo could repeat this story now, in front of the court, it might just help. It could sow some doubts in the minds of jurors and make them wonder if another explanation was possible.

'Pavo, can you tell the court what you witnessed on the night of your master's death?' prompted Gaius.

The guard looked at him for a long moment, then shrugged.

'Nothing,' he said.

Lucius shook inside, like the trembling just before

an earthquake. What was this? What was wrong with Pavo? Had he lost his memory?

Gaius's voice went up a notch, coming close to a squeak: 'What do you mean, *nothing*? Remember what you told Lucius and Quintus the following morning. You told them of a scuffle with an intruder, didn't you?'

Pavo shrugged once more. 'No, I never said anything about that,' he said. 'It was a quiet night as I remember.'

Hearing this, Lucius felt the last of his hopes leaking out of him. He shouldn't have been surprised. Of course Glabrio would have got to Pavo, just as he'd got to everyone else who had worked at their house. Sejanus hadn't bothered to call Pavo to the witness stand because in the new, official version of events, he'd had a 'quiet night', so would have had nothing to report.

With a deep sigh, Gaius told Pavo he could step down. The lawyer grimaced at Lucius, almost as if blaming him for making him look like a fool.

But Lucius wasn't going to give up. He couldn't! A new idea sparked in his brain. Leaning closer, he murmured to Gaius: 'Call in the city prefect, Junius Plautus. He was there that morning and heard Pavo tell us what happened. He'll be able to back us up and prove Pavo's lying.'

Gaius just shook his head and looked sorrowfully at Lucius. 'Junius Plautus is dead,' he whispered back. 'Fishing accident, I think – a few months ago.'

Their case was falling apart. All three of them knew it. Wearily, Gaius approached the praetor and said that he had no more witnesses, but he did have some documentary evidence he'd like to show the court to back up his case.

'What is this *documentary* evidence?' asked the praetor, raising a sceptical eyebrow.

Gaius raised his voice, so the entire courtroom could hear his next words: 'My clients' father was killed because he witnessed the murder of the emperor Titus, and the murderer wished to cover it up. I have documentary evidence proving that Titus was murdered.'

Most of this speech was once again lost behind a wall of jeers and foot-stamping by Glabrio's 'boo-boys'. Gaius continued regardless, until Sejanus interrupted him with a booming voice that quite overwhelmed Gaius's high-pitched, quavering delivery.

'This is pure fantasy,' Sejanus declared, 'and a distraction designed to buy his clients time. Your honour, gentlemen of the jury, the divine Titus was not murdered. He died of a fever, as stated in the autopsy—'

'The autopsy was a fake!' squealed Gaius. 'Glabrio forced him to write it! I have the real—'

But before he could finish, the praetor banged his hammer and shouted at him to be silent.

'I've heard quite enough from you, young man,' said the praetor, spittle forming at the sides of his mouth.

'And I tend to the view of the prosecution that your reference to our beloved former emperor is a ploy, a smokescreen to divert us from the facts.'

Sejanus, with a curl of his lip, then added: 'May I point out that my learned colleague, the counsel for the defence, may have his own interests to protect in this case? After all, is he not under suspicion for the unexplained death of his own father in Ephesus? It's not for me to speculate on such matters, but you do start to wonder whether he may have colluded with his clients in these patricides.'

'This is neither the time nor the place for such hypothesising, counsellor, unless you have evidence to back it up,' said the praetor sharply.

Sejanus bowed his head submissively, and retook his seat. He'd expected the rebuke, but it had achieved its desired effect: calling into question Gaius's integrity.

Gaius, shocked by this underhand tactic, and intimidated by the incessant crowing of Glabrio's handpicked supporters, also retired to his seat. Lucius could see that the young man had been, in so many ways, unprepared for today. He'd been as naïve as Lucius about the justice system, really believing that evidence would be heard and respected, and that witnesses would tell the truth. Today, he had felt the searing touch of raw power and watched the rule of justice melt within its grip. The experience had left him stunned and depressed.

CHAPTER IV

18–19 JULY

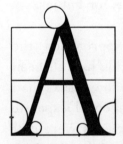fter just a few minutes of deliberation, the jury reached its unanimous verdict, finding Lucius and Quin guilty on all charges. The spectators in the gallery erupted into cheers and applause. Lucius had been expecting this. Even so, the reality was like a crushing sensation in his chest. His legs began wobbling uncontrollably and his throat became very tight. Sweat drenched his palms as he gripped the rail. Quin, by contrast, barely moved. His face was like a mask, with only the working of his jaw muscles betraying his inner turmoil. Lucius knew his brother would go to his death bravely, like a true Roman. He prayed that he would have the strength to do likewise.

When the hubbub had died down, the praetor spoke. Addressing Lucius and Quin, he said: 'The most serious of your crimes is patricide, the killing of your father, and your punishment will reflect that. According to Lex Pompeia de Parricidiis,* the penalty for patricide is the poena cullei, the punishment of the sack.'

'No! No! No!' Lucius couldn't prevent the cries of raw fear escaping his throat. He'd heard of the punishment of the sack, of course – who hadn't? It was the worst thing – the worst thing imaginable.

He felt a steely grip on his arm. It was Quin. 'Be brave, brother,' he told him. 'Be brave, for Father.'

'Mask them!' ordered the praetor.

Soldiers with wolfskin masks approached the defendants. Lucius knew then that this had all been planned in advance by Glabrio – the masks had been brought to the trial for this moment. Desperate now, he sought out his mother. Her eyes were cast down towards her hands, which were fidgeting with something in her lap. 'Mother!' screamed Lucius. 'Tell them the truth. Tell them we didn't–' He couldn't finish. A soldier grabbed him by the neck and shoved the wolfskin over his face. It smelled musty and rotten and made him choke. The sudden immersion in darkness reminded him of times in the past when he'd put on a gladiator helmet – only this time there

* *Lex Pompeia de Parricidiis: the law of Gnaeus Pompeius concerning those who murder their relatives.*

were no eye holes to see through, and the air stank
and was scarcely breathable. Inside a Hoplomachus*
helmet there had always been hope. Inside a wolfskin,
there was none.

Iron manacles closed once again over his wrists,
rubbing painfully against the tender flesh. Rough
hands tore his sandals off and forced hard wooden
clogs onto his feet. As he was pushed and prodded out
of the enclosure, he heard the praetor's solemn voice:
'According to our ancient traditions, they have been
masked and their feet bound in wood, so the air may
no longer be defiled by their breath, nor the ground by
their tread.'

Taunting heckles and catcalls rained down on them
as they walked. Something soft and wet slammed into
Lucius's ear. He could feel it dripping down his tunic.
The clogs pinched his toes and scraped the soles of
his feet. They made clip-clopping echoes like horses'
hooves as he was led across the marble floor. But this
was nothing – this was just the beginning. He didn't
want to think about what lay ahead.

He knew they were outside by the July afternoon
heat on his skin and the sudden change in the
soundscape. Gone were the echoes of his feet on marble
and the jeers of Glabrio's supporters. Instead, he was
assailed by the ordinary noises of the Forum: shouts of
vendors and Senate criers and declamations of lawyers
pleading their cases; a flutter of pigeons, the sizzle of

* *Hoplomachus: a gladiator dressed as a Greek infantryman.*

frying meat, the laughter of spectators entertained by a street performer. All of it so ordinary, so everyday – the eternal city was carrying on, as it always did and always would. The deaths of the Valerii boys, and of their once great family, would make no difference to anyone in the end.

Lucius felt a hard shove in his back and he stumbled forward. 'Get a move on, scum!' a coarse voice yelled in his ear. He almost tumbled down the Basilica steps until a hand closed painfully on his arm and jerked him upright. The hand didn't let go, yanking and pulling him along the cobbles, until he was back in the Tullianum. He was then forced at frightening speed down the stairwell, his feet scrabbling to maintain purchase on the steep, twisting steps. Deeper they went, and he felt the subterranean chill and the ancient stench of fear closing around him like a giant fist. This was the deepest pit of Hades, he decided, as he was pushed into his cell and heard the clank and squeak of a door closing and a key turning in a rusty lock. The chill and the dampness began to seep into his bones. Nothing could be worse than this. *Nothing!*

Except what was going to happen next…

He was lying on the floor. Quin was nearby. He could hear him breathing.

'You know what we're facing, don't you?' Lucius said. Horrific images had been crowding his head ever since the praetor had announced their fate. He had to talk about it, share it, or he'd go mad. 'The punishment of the sack, it's–'

'Hush,' said Quin. 'Don't think about it. Let's just enjoy our last night alive. Let's think about the good times. Remember… Remember that time, Lu, when we caught the raven with a bird net.'

They'd been climbing trees in a forest near their house when they saw it – big and proud, sitting on a branch of a sapling. They'd crouched for long minutes, still as cats, watching and waiting for their chance. When it hopped down to the grass, Quin had dived. He'd always been exceptionally quick.

'*It* caught *me*, more like,' said Lucius, recalling the pain of the raven's hard, shiny beak snapping shut on his hand while Quin struggled to keep the net closed.

The bird must have been sick, or else they couldn't have caught it – so their tutor, Agathon, had said when they brought it to him. For a sick bird it was lively, still snapping at them with its vicious beak. They wanted to keep it, train it like a hawk. But Agathon had made them let it go – told them that you can't keep a wild bird captive, and they should let it enjoy its last days in peace. He remembered watching it fly away, low over the trees. He wished he could fly away now.

The boys had precious few shared memories. They hadn't often played together, being so different in character. Quin was always out in the woods, trying to trap animals or whittle wooden weapons, or playing war games with his friends. As for Lucius, when he wasn't out walking his trusty dog Argos, he could usually be found in the library, reading a scroll or talking with his father. He recalled the hazy afternoon sun coming through the library window, glittering in the dust motes, and the sweet, dry scent of papyrus, and the gentle voice of his father relating tales of ancient battles and heroes, of Alexander, Hannibal, Scipio and Caesar. The memory filled him with almost unbearable nostalgia.

Quin continued to reminisce, and Lucius listened, even though half the things his brother spoke of he couldn't recall – perhaps Quin imagined Lucius had been there when he hadn't. Still, Quin's stories acted as a kind of softening screen behind which his mind could hide for a while from the awful reality of their circumstances. Inside the stuffy darkness of the wolfskin, he could pretend he wasn't in a cell awaiting gruesome execution, but in the happier realms of his childhood.

At length, they heard footsteps and the grinding clink of the door being opened. Lucius's heart stood still. Fear knifed through his ribs. It was too soon! They couldn't have prepared the punishment yet.

But it was only Gaius, come to say goodbye.

Lucius could hear the sob in the young lawyer's throat. 'They'll come for me next,' he whimpered as he held Lucius's hand. 'You heard Sejanus's threat. They'll pin my father's death on me, just as they did with you.'

'While there's life, there's hope,' said Lucius. It was

bizarre, considering their relative situations, but he felt the need to comfort Gaius. 'You must keep fighting to the end. Do you still have the documents?'

'No,' said Gaius with a snivel. 'They took them from me. Of course, I should have expected that! The only reason they lured us into a courtroom fight was because they knew I'd have to bring along the autopsy report. Glabrio will take great pleasure in destroying the last remaining evidence of his foul crimes.'

Lucius's heart sagged on hearing this. He thought he'd plumbed the depths of wretchedness, but there always seemed further to fall. 'So we travelled two thousand miles and risked our lives for nothing,' he muttered.

'I'm sorry,' cried Gaius. 'I believed in the fairness of our justice system. Today, I was proved tragically wrong.'

'You did your best,' said Quin, 'and for that we thank you. The justice system *should* be fair. In the hands of the right leaders, it would be. But we live in bad times, my friend. Everything has become corrupted. Don't blame yourself.'

Gaius couldn't reply. He was too full of emotion.

Lucius knew this would be the last chance he'd ever have to talk to Gaius. He felt a growing pressure to unburden himself of something that still pricked at his conscience. 'Gaius,' he said. 'I have to tell you about your father, about his death.'

He heard Gaius's sharp intake of breath and could

almost imagine the sudden awakening of interest in the boy's tearful eyes. 'What is it?' Gaius asked in a tight voice.

'I led the killer to your father's hideout. I didn't realise we were being followed. If it hadn't been for me, your father might... he might still be alive.'

There was a long silence. Lucius felt his hand being released. The chill of the room seemed to grow even deeper, more desolate. 'I'm sorry,' Lucius said at length, disturbed by Gaius's lack of response. 'Please forgive me.'

Then he felt the boy's hand again, tighter than before. 'It's OK,' murmured Gaius in a flat voice. 'It wasn't your fault. I'm glad you managed to see my father. There is nothing to forgive.'

Shortly afterwards, Gaius was informed by the guards that his time was up. When he had gone, Lucius and Quin lapsed into their own private thoughts. The hours passed, only a few of them spent in fitful sleep. It was hard to find rest with the cramped feeling in his clog-bound feet and the soreness of his manacled wrists. In the long wakeful periods, Lucius desperately fended off thoughts of what was to come by pondering those dearest to him. Val would grow into a beauty for sure, and no doubt be married off to the son of a wealthy senator. She would be OK, so long as she suppressed her wilder side and played the role of dutiful wife and mother. He and Quin would soon be just a memory to her. As she grew older, their brief rebellion would come to seem like some absurd yet exciting childhood adventure. As for Isi, he prayed she was safe, and hadn't been captured and killed for trying to incite the Roman mob. He hoped she would survive this and go on to live a happy life – maybe go into business with her friend Faustina, or return to her life as a roving gladiator with Hierax and the Swords of Isis.

When the soldiers came for them, Lucius was dozing, and the urgent clatter of iron-soled sandals on stone steps was sudden and brutal in his ears. He and Quin were hauled roughly up the stairs and Lucius bit back a cry as his shin scraped once, twice, three times against the sharp angle of the steps. Soon they were back in the open air of the Forum. Beneath the stink of the wolfskin hood, Lucius could smell fresh-baked bread. It was morning. But his guts were so twisted up with fear, he had no appetite for bread or anything else. The sneering heckles of Glabrio's rented mob sounded like the bleats and honks of farmyard animals. Nearby, he could hear the snort of some real animals – horses.

Soldiers pushed the boys into the back of an open wagon. Lucius crawled forward on his elbows and tried to curl up into a ball. He wished he could block his ears against the mockery and insults being flung at them – he wished he could die right here and now, before the real horror began. The wagon lurched forward across the cobbles. They were heading south – he could guess that much – skirting the southern flanks of the Capitoline Hill, heading for the Campus Martius and the Tiber, where the punishment of the sack always took place. The wagon swayed. Lucius's stomach clenched. His mind was a chaos of swirling fish-like thoughts, no sooner formed than gone, and engulfing them all was a paralysing, ever-tightening net of fear.

The crowd followed them every step of their slow progress, baying at their heels. At last, he could hear, above the catcalls, the lapping of water against the riverbank, and he knew they had reached their destination. The wagon drew to a halt and, moments later, rough, callused hands were laid on his limbs and he was dragged away. Lucius felt himself being carried a short distance, then raised up on some sort of platform. His tunic was ripped from his body, leaving him exposed but for his loincloth. His arms, still bound at the wrists, were wrenched painfully upwards, almost tearing them from their sockets. His chest was squashed against a fat wooden post. He tried to go up on tiptoes to take the pressure off his arms, but his feet, in their wooden prisons, would not rise. Just as the pain in his shoulders seemed to grow unbearable, the pressure eased and his manacled wrists slid down the other side of the post, securing him tightly to it.

He tried to imagine that all this was happening to

someone else – that he was actually somewhere far away. But the chanting, the laughter, the stench, the taste of spit and vomit in his mouth, were all too raw and intense; however much he wanted to escape, these sensations kept dragging him back.

This is not the worst, his vicious mind kept whispering to him. *The worst is yet to come.*

He heard a swishing sound and then *crack!* A line of hot agony lit up his back. The air shuddered. He screamed. Vomit filled the wolfskin hood.

Crack! Harder this time. His skin felt as though it was burning – literally on fire.

Crack! The third stroke was laid upon the already searing line of the first. Lucius didn't think such pain was even possible.

The strokes were coming faster now – all over his back and even on his legs. They felt like sharp knives slicing into him, gradually cutting him into sections. He had a mental picture of his back as one massive wound, with mounds of puffy pink flesh criss-crossed by lines of blood. The wait before each blow was the worst of it. Where and when would the next one fall? Animal noises spewed from his mouth: groans of fear and self-pity interspersed with screams of pain. His mind had become jelly – incapable of thought. And all the time, in some small part of his brain, a voice kept repeating: *This is not the worst… The worst is yet to come.*

Finally, the beatings ceased. He waited and waited, hardly daring to hope that this part of his ordeal might be over – his body throbbed in the agony of its many sores and trembled with fear that the torturer was merely pausing to catch his breath. When another stroke failed to come he began sobbing with relief, even though the rational part of him knew that this was just the prelude. *The worst was yet to come.*

A voice – it sounded like the praetor's – cut through the fog of his confusion. The voice was like the mournful call of a funeral horn. The words, with their solemn finality, impaled him like spears. *This was the end. The worst was coming now…*

'Quintus Valerius Felix, Lucius Valerius Aquila,' intoned the praetor. 'You took the life of the one who gave you life. And so it is decreed that you shall face the punishment of the sack – the reverse of being born. The sack is another womb, but instead of nurturing you, this womb will kill you…'

As the voice went on, other sounds began to percolate through Lucius's dazed consciousness: yapping, squawking, hissing sounds. And beyond these, a distant howling, as of a twisting, billowing wind, that seemed to be growing slowly louder.

'Placed in the sack with you,' continued the voice, 'will be three live animals: a dog – an animal all people look down upon; a chicken – which, like yourselves, is devoid of all affection for its parents; and a serpent – whose birth is said to cause its mother's death. You will be placed in the sack with these three animals and the sack will be sewn up and then cast into the river. Thus you shall be denied the elements of air for life, and earth for interment after death. That is your punishment.'*

Lucius had already known what to expect, but hearing it spelled out was almost impossible to bear. He couldn't imagine the horror of being squeezed into a sack with these frightened animals, and sinking into the cold, dark, suffocating waters of the Tiber as the frenzied creatures bit and scratched at his wounds.

He was so benumbed with fright that he failed at first to notice that something odd was happening in the world outside his wolfskin mask – something no one could have anticipated. If he'd been listening more closely, he'd have heard the praetor's voice stammer slightly towards the close of his speech and speed up to get to the end. He'd have noticed that the baiting and jeering of Glabrio's supporters had completely stopped, and that the howling wind-like noise he'd heard earlier had now massively increased in volume and had splintered into thousands of individual voices and a rumbling crescendo of running feet. A crowd, he suddenly realised, was converging on them – a huge and very angry crowd.

The praetor spoke again, trying to sound calm, but now clearly panicked: 'Guards! Disperse that mob! Use whatever force is necessary!' But his voice

---

* This is a genuine punishment, described by the Roman writer Cicero in the 1st century BC. More detail is given in the Digest, a summary of Roman law compiled for the emperor Justinian the Great in the 6th century AD.

sounded like the cheeping of a sparrow in the swirling cacophony of rage now engulfing them.

There were screams and grunts as the guards around them were kicked, punched and struck down. Lucius felt someone's panting breath close to his cheek. An axe blade whistled through the air. There was a clink of breaking metal and the post he was attached to shook. His arms, no longer forced to embrace the post, fell back to his sides. He was free! Someone had chopped through the chain of his wrist manacles. The wolfskin mask was ripped from his head and he had to squeeze his eyes shut against the blinding light.

A familiar voice shouted into his ear: 'Some of the witnesses have started denying their stories! It's official! The trial wasn't fair!'

Lucius felt dizzy. It was hard to take in what was happening. It sounded like Isi who had just spoken. Could it be her? It seemed impossible. He began to wobble and thought he was going to fall, until someone caught him and brought him gently down to the ground. He cried out as his lacerated back touched earth, and his rescuer quickly turned him so he was lying on his stomach. As his eyes adjusted to the light, he began to take in the immediate scene. Quin was lying next to him, also on his stomach, his back a bleeding mess. Arrayed on the ground nearby were unconscious and bleeding soldiers, one of them holding a rod dripping with blood. Two small dogs were barking at each other. A chicken was clucking somewhere.

Only then did Lucius notice that someone was holding his hand. He craned his neck upwards, squinting through the dazzle of sunlight. It was Isi, smiling at him. Tears spilled from his eyes. He squeezed her hand tight, but couldn't find words. His back was still a writhing snakepit of pain. Isi held a cup of water to his lips and he drank gratefully. Then her attention was diverted by something happening on Lucius's right. He turned to see the river filled up with small boats. On one of them was the praetor, his clothes and hair in disarray, bleeding from a cut on his cheek, being rowed away through the traffic by a small team of anxious-looking lictors,* while people on the bank and in nearby boats shook their fists and bellowed angry threats at him.

A far bigger mass of people surrounded Lucius and Quin on the landward side. All that prevented them from coming even closer was a cordon of burly men with linked arms. The crowd was roaring its excitement, the nearest ones pointing at Quin and smiling with joyous amazement. Some were straining to reach through the cordon so they could touch him. Lucius could hear people shouting: 'The Phoenix of Pompeii! It's him! He's alive! He's really alive!'

Gaius appeared next to them, almost bouncing with elation. 'The prosecution case has virtually collapsed,' he shouted. 'Vedrix, the slave who said he saw Quin stabbing his father, has now confessed that he lied.

* *lictors: bodyguards.*

89

Then Pavo came forward and admitted that he *had*, in fact, had a tussle with a tattooed intruder. When the news got out about this, there was a near-riot in the Forum. The crowd went mad when they heard that their hero, Quin, and his brother, Lucius, hadn't received a fair trial!'

'The crowd?' murmured Quin through cracked lips. 'We saw no crowd – except for Glabrio's rent-a-mob.'

Gaius turned to Isi, eyes aglow with admiration. 'Isidora assembled them this morning.'

'How did you do it?' asked Quin.

'*You* did it, Quin,' she replied. 'Your name did it. All I did was persuade fifty men and women from Suburra to follow me into the Forum. When they got there and they heard from the Senate criers about the trial, the news spread like Mercury* through all the tenements and back streets of their neighbourhood. People raced to the Forum, overjoyed that the Phoenix was still alive, but worried that you might be snatched from them before they got to see you. Most wanted to march straight here, to the Campus Martius, but the gang leaders, who have a lot of influence on the streets, told the crowd that if Quin had killed his father, he should face the consequences. I tried to argue with them. I told them that you two had been framed, but I quickly realised that the gang leaders had been bought off by Glabrio. They would never have moved against

* *Mercury: the messenger of the gods, often shown with winged hat and sandals to symbolise his speed.*

him, not even for Quin. Then Vedrix and Pavo came forward and admitted they'd lied, and after that there was nothing the gang leaders or anyone could have done to stop the stampede onto the Campus Martius. It was like a human tide, a force of nature – nothing could have stopped them.'

Lucius looked again at the sea of smiling, laughing faces, and at the line of men puffing and straining to keep them at bay.

'You're amazing, Isi,' he managed to croak.

She gave a modest half-smile. 'Luckily, on the way here, one of the gang leaders saw sense and came over to our side. He provided this cordon of tough guys. Otherwise, the crowd might have crushed you.'

At that moment they heard the blast of a horn and a pounding of hoofbeats. Above the heads of the multitude, the white crests of mounted Praetorians could be glimpsed converging on the scene from at least three different directions. There were cries of confusion and distress, and the crowd immediately began to scatter. The ones who were slow to disperse or opted to stand their ground received clouts from oval shields or the flats of swords, or, worse, were trampled beneath horses' hooves.

Lucius's mood quickly plummeted from dazed relief and joy to the pits of despair. It seemed that not even the ordinary people of Rome could save them from the dreadful omnipotence of Glabrio. Within minutes, the exuberant throngs of Suburrans were gone, their chants and songs merely echoes on the wind, and this stretch of riverside was filled instead with the silent, menacing ranks of armoured men and horses.

It didn't take long for the praetor to make his return to the scene, surrounded by at least fifteen lictors. He had tidied up his toga and his hair and a dressing had been applied to his cheek. Accompanying him were the senators who had comprised the jury at the trial, all with their own contingents of bodyguards. It seemed that no one was taking any chances with their personal security after such an outbreak of mob violence. There was no sign of Glabrio or Caecilia.

Lucius fully expected the praetor to order the continuation of their execution, so he was stunned to hear him announce: 'New evidence has come to light with regard to the Valerii case. I have discussed the matter with the jury, and they have decided to retract the guilty verdict for patricide.' Hearing this, Lucius was filled with ecstatic relief, but the smile froze on his face as the praetor continued: 'However, the conviction for the crimes of murdering the messenger Ennius and mutilating Tribune Lurco, as well as the lesser offences of impersonation, still stand.' The praetor now turned to address Lucius and Quin directly. 'I have therefore decided,' he said, 'to commute your sentence to damnatio ad gladium* – you will be killed by a sword in the arena. You must fight without shield or armour.'

---

* *damnatio ad gladium: condemnation to the sword.*

'This is execution by another name!' Gaius yelled angrily.

Quin merely gritted his teeth. 'At least there'll be some honour in it.'

PART TWO

DAMNATIO AD GLADIUM

CHAPTER V

'I thought I'd seen the last of you two,' grunted Crassus. The short, stocky lanista* of the Ludus Romanus eyed Lucius and Quin from behind his desk. His craggy face creased into a smile that could almost be considered friendly, except that his eyes remained as hard and cold as obsidian.

'The pleasure is entirely mutual,' smiled Quin. It had only been two days since he'd been beaten half to death, but his natural cheeky charm hadn't taken long to resurface.

'I heard you were both dead,' said Crassus.

'It's a long story,' said Lucius. He found it hard to stand up, and he kept one hand on the table for

* lanista: trainer.

97

support. His back and legs were still extremely tender.

'Don't bore me with it,' said Crassus with a dismissive wave of the hand. 'All that's important is that you're now both damnati ad gladium. So your return to this ludus will be short and not exactly sweet.'

Quin let his eyes wander through the window of Crassus's shabby little office to the quadrangle outside where weeds were sprouting up through the dust. 'You've let things slide, Crassus,' he said amiably. 'This place is becoming a dump.'

'I'll have none of your lip, Quintus Felix,' harrumphed Crassus. 'You may have been a big star once, and perhaps you still have a few fans out there in the slums, but in here you're nothing. Zero. Get it?'

'Glad to see you've lost none of your motivational skills,' smirked Quin.

'Shut it!' Crassus scowled. He placed his heavy fists on the table. 'Just to make things clear, you have no status here, either of you. You're not going to see or associate with the other gladiators except at mealtimes and training. The rest of the time, you'll be locked in your cell. And don't expect any privileges in training either, Quintus, just because of who you once were. You're both starting at the bottom rung – the equivalent of tirones.'*

He surveyed their scars and strained postures, and gave a resigned snort. 'You can have a few weeks'

* tirones: beginners.

grace to recover from your wounds, and then you'll go straight into hard training for the Ludi Romani.* Now get out of here.'

After leaving Crassus's office, Lucius and Quin limped back to the medical room so that the doctor could change the dressings on their wounds. It was a daily ordeal for them. Fortunately, the doctor was Aelius Eumenes, a familiar, friendly face from their original spell at the ludus. Eumenes gently removed the bandages on Quin's back, while Lucius leaned against a nearby wall and waited his turn.

'The bruising is progressing nicely through its stages,' commented the doctor.

'Pleased to hear it,' muttered Quin.

'He's black and blue,' observed Lucius.

'Yes, it's certainly a pleasing sight,' nodded Eumenes. 'And in a few days the bruises will turn a greenish colour, then yellowy brown – the final stage before they're fully healed.'

He picked up a pad of ram's wool, which he dipped in some fat and a decoction of herbs and spices including rue, borage, plantain, yarrow and cinnamon, and then applied it to the bruising. 'This should speed up the healing process,' he said.

* *Ludi Romani: the Roman Games, an annual festival held in September, in honour of Jupiter, the father of the gods.*

'No acid vinegar today?' asked Quin with a relieved sigh.

'The wounds are clean now,' murmured Eumenes. 'They just need to be helped on their way.'

The doctor looked much less pleased when he uncovered the bruising on the back of Quin's thigh. He gave the wound a hard tap, making Quin yelp. 'This bruise is still firm and very swollen,' said the doctor. 'It's not healing properly. I'm going to have to drain it.'

Lucius watched through squinting eyes and parted fingers as Eumenes inserted the sharp tip of a scalpel blade into the swollen area and let the trapped blood flow out. The doctor pressed a clean swab to the wound and then rebandaged Quin's legs and back.

After he'd finished with Quin, Eumenes turned his attention to Lucius, and here the story was much the same: everything was healing well, except for one problematic injury – this time to Lucius's lower back. Lucius had already sensed there was something wrong there. It felt tighter and more tender than anywhere else. The skin had split, and the wound had become infected. Eumenes went to work on the other bruises first, before treating the infected one with a lotion made up of lard, honey and lint.

'It's a funny thing, infection,' he said as he worked. 'For centuries, physicians have been trying to work out what causes it. Could it be swamp gas? Bad air? Rotting vegetation? One of the strangest theories I ever heard came from a scholar called Marcus Terentius Varro, who lived more than a hundred years ago. He claimed that infections were caused by miniature creatures too small for the eye to see, which floated around in the air and entered the body through the mouth and nose, or through cuts like this. Can you imagine!'

After their visit to the treatment room, Lucius and Quin hobbled their way over to the dining hall for their midday meal. Lucius couldn't help noticing the damp patches on the walls, as well as the peeling paint. Quin had been right: the ludus *was* turning into a dump. The long tables that ran the length of the dining hall were filled with ravenous gladiators all intent on spooning down their barley broth as fast as possible. Not one of them looked up as Quin entered.

This was their second day at the ludus, and Lucius was now used to this complete lack of reaction to his brother. If Quin had initially expected to be welcomed as a returning hero by his old familia, he'd have been disappointed. There had been a substantial turnover of fighters since he'd last set foot in the school over two years earlier, and few remembered him, except by reputation. Besides, gladiators were not, by nature, hero-worshipping types. Most of them were either hardened criminals, prisoners of war or unruly slaves with no respect for anyone, least of all their fellow inmates. Within the ranks of the sixty-strong familia, there were also fifteen auctorati – citizens who had volunteered to become gladiators. They were a mix of glory seekers, rebels, social misfits and men who'd simply fallen on hard times, and it was towards this group that Lucius and Quin naturally gravitated.

They made their way over to where three of these auctorati were seated together and took their places next to them. Lucius seated himself awkwardly, putting the weight on his less bruised buttock. Hector, the biggest of the auctorati, was a blue-eyed, blond Secutor.* The son of a freedman who'd grown wealthy as an importer of garum sauce, Hector had defied his father's hopes of continuing in the family business and opted instead for a life of action – initially as a legionary. After being thrown out of the army for insubordination, he'd reinvented himself as a gladiator and earned spectacular success in the arena. He was now primus palus – the highest-ranking gladiator at the ludus.

Hector was in full flow when Lucius and Quin joined them. 'Who's won the most fights in Rome? I have. Fact! Who's won the most fights in Italia? I have. Fact! Who's the most successful Secutor currently on the circuit? I am. Fact!' The Secutor stabbed the air with his forefinger with every *Fact!* 'So don't try teaching me your fancy moves, Hilario, because I know every trick in the book. I *wrote* the book! I know what you're

* Secutor: 'Pursuer', a gladiator armed with a short sword (gladius), infantry shield and fully enclosed helmet.

going to do before you've even thought of it. I'm three moves ahead of you. I've already got my sword pinned to your throat before you've even got your helmet on.'

'How do you know you've won the most fights in Italia?' asked one of his companions, Hilario.

'How?' frowned Hector, his mouth now a perfect circle of astonishment at this questioning of his 'facts'. 'Because Crassus told me, that's how. Crassus is in touch with the lanistae of loads of other schools and they're always comparing notes. I'm at the top of every list. Fact!'

'Perhaps you haven't met Quintus Felix, then,' said Hilario, with a nod towards Quin. Hilario was a sandy-haired, broken-nosed Provocator* – almost as big as Hector, but with a much more easy-going manner. He was one of the few who remembered Quin from his first period at the ludus two years earlier. 'Quintus was the best fighter in our familia while he was here,' said Hilario. 'Maybe the best we've ever had.'

Hector let his cold blue eyes play over Quin's scarred and bent body. 'I find that hard to believe,' he said. 'Did you ever make primus palus?'

'No,' said Quin. A slave had arrived with two more bowls of barley broth and he and Lucius began tucking in.

'You would have, though, if you'd been here longer – that's what I heard,' said the third auctoratus, a young, brown-skinned tiro with tousled black hair,

---

* Provocator: 'Challenger', a gladiator with similar equipment to a Secutor, but with more body armour.

called Sergius. 'If you hadn't given up on being a gladiator so soon, you'd have made primus palus for sure.'

'I wasn't interested,' said Quin simply. 'The thought of killing people for sport sickened me then, and it sickens me now.'

'That sounds like a lame excuse,' said Hector. 'You lost your nerve, more like. A real gladiator is a gladiator for life. Fact! I take all-comers. You won't find me running away when the going gets tough. That's why I made primus palus and you didn't. Fact!'

Quin continued to eat his broth in silence.

Lucius sipped at his, though it made him grimace. 'This is disgusting,' he said under his breath.

'Too right it is,' said Hilario. 'No flavour, mostly water. They wouldn't even feed this stuff to animals.' He dropped his spoon, letting it splash into his soup, and called out to a nearby guard. 'You wouldn't even feed this stuff to animals!'

The guard ignored him.

'This place has gone to the dogs since Glabrio took it over,' Hilario continued in a lower voice. 'The food tastes like watery manure, the leisure periods are getting shorter, and the exercise and training sessions are getting tougher and longer. He runs the place on a shoestring, and expects to turn out fighters to beat the best in the peninsula…'

'We *are* the best in the peninsula,' said Hector between slurps of his broth. 'Or at least I am.'

While the other gladiators headed out for their afternoon training session, Lucius and Quin were marched under guard back to their cell. They were excused exercise and training until they'd recovered from their injuries, but as damnati ad gladium this effectively meant almost permanent confinement to their cells. Apart from for washing, eating and medical treatment, the only time they were allowed out was for an hour at dusk in the quad while the other gladiators were in the bathhouse. Quin limped around the cramped, dark room like a caged predator from the African savanna. 'Why can't they at least let us watch the others train?' he growled. 'I need space! Light! Air!'

Lucius curled up on his straw mattress, putting the weight on his less painful injuries. 'I'd stay clear of that Hector fellow once we start training,' he said. 'Now he knows you were a big star here once, he'll want to prove a point by humiliating you.'

'I've met guys like that before,' said Quin. 'The ones who keep talking themselves up are secretly scared. They're always worrying that some newcomer's going to sneak up and steal their crown.'

'And I suppose you think that newcomer's going to be you?'

Quin shook his head. 'I'm not interested in that kind of glory any more. I don't want to be primus palus…

Though I wouldn't mind wiping the smug look off his face.'

'Remember what Crassus said,' warned Lucius. 'We've got no status here now. We don't want to make things worse for ourselves.'

'How could things be any worse?' asked Quin. 'We're going to die in the arena soon anyway.'

'I just can't believe there's no hope,' said Lucius, shaking his head. 'We survived the punishment of the sack, didn't we? Gaius and Isi are still out there. They'll come up with a plan, I'm sure of it. We just need to keep our heads down and survive the next few weeks. And that means keeping out of trouble.'

This made Quin smile. 'But I love trouble, and trouble loves me. I was born to make trouble. Who's the biggest troublemaker in Italia? I am.' Chuckling, he thumped the air with his forefinger. 'Fact!'

The weeks crawled by, and each day followed the same dreary routine: breakfast; back to the cell; medical room; back to the cell; lunch; back to the cell; exercise in the quad; back to the cell; bathhouse; back to the cell; supper; back to the cell. Quin griped and complained through all of it, which was his way of dealing with the boredom and frustration.

Lucius, meanwhile, kept his head down, said little, and put all his energy into the simple task of surviving.

To cheer himself up, he often thought back to that golden day at Lake Albano. He spread his hands across the dirty straw mattress and tried to remember the feel of Isi's body when they embraced in the water. He closed his eyes, and the night wind coming through the cell window was her sweet breath against his cheek. In his current miserable state, that day stood out as something perfect, like a gleam of light in a dark cave. He wondered if Isi ever thought back to that moment. Had it meant anything to her?

Gradually, they recovered from their wounds. The bruises vanished, the cuts healed, the swellings subsided and the pains eased. Light exercise and training sessions were added to their routine, and they began to partake a little more in the regular life of the familia. Finally, a few days after the Ides of August[*] and about four weeks after the boys' arrival at the ludus, Eumenes pronounced them both fully fit.

By this time, the school was in a ferment of activity with the approach of the Roman Games, starting in early September. Leisure time was cut even further to allow more time for training. All leave was cancelled for the auctorati, so they found themselves confined to the ludus, like every other gladiator. An atmosphere of surly resentment settled over the school, which was particularly noticeable at meal times. Usually, the only good thing about an approaching games was that the food tended to get better, with more meat and

[*] *Ides of August: the 13th of August.*

fresh fruit added to the gladiators' diet to build up
their strength and energy. But the food didn't get any
better at the Ludus Romanus – not this time – it was
the same bland barley and vegetable broth each day,
supplemented by a disgusting brew containing bone
ash, to strengthen bones. The gladiators, particularly
Hilario, complained bitterly.

As damnati ad gladium, Lucius and Quin were
the lowest of the low – ranked even beneath their
fellow criminals in the hierarchy of the familia. All the
other criminals at the school were damnati ad ludos
(condemned to the games), which was a lot better than
being condemned to death as Lucius and Quin were,
and could even be the start of a promising career for
those with a little talent.

Because of their lowly status, Quin and Lucius were
ordered to train with the most unpromising novicii* –
slaves imported from Germania and Britannia with
no fighting skills and seemingly no desire to learn any
either. They weren't even equipped with a manica or
a greave for arm and leg protection, and the wooden
swords they were forced to fight with were the chipped
and broken cast-offs of more senior gladiators.

Despite these handicaps, the brothers were
delighted to be out in the fresh air again, moving
freely and feeling their bodies gain in strength. Lucius
guessed that the novicii they were training with had
been earmarked by Crassus as Gregarii, the most

* *novicii: novices, complete beginners with no training.*

expendable form of fighter, used mainly as sword and axe fodder in battle re-enactments. The ludus hadn't paid much for them, and Crassus certainly wasn't going to waste his resources by training them, as they weren't expected to last long.

As a result, Quin and Lucius soon found themselves in the role of teachers, attempting to educate the novicii in the art of swordfighting. It was tough, because their students could barely speak any Latin and didn't really want to learn anyway. They had been farmers, bakers and craftsmen in their former lives, and most had never held a sword before. In the end, the best their trainers could do was offer them a few basic moves that might just extend their survival time in the arena to more than a few panic-stricken seconds.

The brothers would first demonstrate a new strike, parry or counterstrike against each other, while their bemused pupils stood around in a circle, eyes agog. Then they would ask each novicius to step forward in turn and try it for themselves. These first efforts were invariably fumbling and floppy-wristed, but in time, and with the help of further demonstrations, they gradually improved. When Lucius and Quin were sure that their charges were reasonably proficient in that move, they would let them loose to practise on each other or on a wooden palus.*

* palus: a post planted in the ground to be used as a practice target.

One day, about a week after they'd begun these training sessions, a surprising thing happened. Lucius and Quin were in the middle of demonstrating how a shield could be used as a second weapon to open up an opponent's defences when they were interrupted by a shout.

'Quintus Felix!'

They stopped and looked up. Standing about ten paces away from them was the primus palus himself – Hector. He was surrounded by a gang of beefy-looking friends and admirers. They were all auctorati, the elite of the school. Lucius was surprised that Hector was even deigning to address Quin. Since that initial encounter in the dining hall, the primus palus had completely ignored him as one might a dog in the street (and he'd ignored Lucius as if he were a flea on that dog). All the other auctorati – apart from Hilario and Sergius, who remained friendly – had followed suit and begun to snub them. The brothers had taken the hint and now seated themselves among the lower-ranked gladiators in the dining hall.

So what was going on? Lucius immediately had a bad feeling about this, like a tingling in his scalp. He didn't like the way Hector was looking at Quin.

'Quintus Felix, you were hot stuff once, or so people keep telling me,' said Hector. He had his sword in his hands and was gently weaving it through the air in front of him, causing ripples in his impressive chest and shoulder muscles. 'But then apparently you got scared and went off to fight animals instead. And when that got too scary for you, you started racing chariots. It's not exactly an impressive career, is it, Quintus? Even so, people keep saying I should fight you, I don't know why. They say you're some sort of legend. Well, there's only room for one legend in this school, and that's me. I'm the best here. Fact! I'm the best there's ever been. Fact! And I don't like the way people keep mentioning your name whenever I remind them of this. It's getting on my nerves. So fight me, Quintus Felix. Fight me, so I can prove all these doubters wrong.'

'I don't want to fight you,' said Quin. He turned away from Hector and resumed his former position opposite his brother. Lucius was pleasantly surprised. It wasn't like Quin to turn down a challenge. Maybe he'd listened to Lucius's warning, after all, and had decided to stay out of trouble.

Hector suddenly darted forward and gave Quin a shove, sending him sprawling face down in the dirt.

'Scared, are you?' sneered the primus palus. 'Scared I might tarnish your legend by showing these people what a loser you actually are?'

Quin took his time getting to his feet and dusting himself down. He looked up at Hector and said: 'I'm not scared. I just don't want to fight you. I'm busy here, teaching these good people, and now you're interrupting me.'

Hector's eyes narrowed. He grabbed Quin by the scruff of his tunic and pulled him closer. He was a lot taller than Quin, and he forced Quin's head back with his other hand so he could look him in the face. 'No one refuses a challenge from me,' snarled Hector. 'Be at the training arena in five minutes. If you're not there, I'll come for your brother – send him for another long spell in the medical room. I hear Eumenes specialises in mending broken bones.'

Hector returned to his friends, leaving Quin shaking his head in bemusement.

'You mustn't do this,' advised Lucius.

'I don't want him hurting you,' Quin replied.

'I can look after myself.'

Quin watched as a slave handed Hector his Secutor helmet and shield. 'Not against him you can't,' he said. 'I'll take him. This won't take long.' He turned to Lucius. 'Go and see if you can find me some Retiarius* kit from the armoury.'

Lucius stared at him for a moment before racing away, his heart pounding.

Five minutes later, Secutor and Retiarius faced each other in the training arena – a miniature amphitheatre, complete with tiered spectator seating, located near one end of the quad. A dozen or so of Hector's friends and stooges filled the front row on one side of

---

* *Retiarius: a gladiator who fights with net (rete) and trident, the traditional opponent of a Secutor.*

the arena. Lucius sat alone on the other side, Quin's sole supporter.

Suddenly, Crassus entered the arena. 'What's going on?' he shouted, red-faced and with eyes of thunder. 'Why aren't you lot training? Get back to the quad, all of you – now!'

There were groans of disappointment from the auctorati in the seats as they climbed to their feet. Then Hector took off his helmet, and Crassus's face immediately softened.

'Oh, it's you,' he said.

'I only need a few minutes, lanista,' Hector said sweetly. 'Just want to teach this kid a lesson he won't forget. Can you let my friends stay and watch? Please?'

Crassus frowned. He appeared uneasy, but no longer exactly angry. He nodded reluctantly. 'OK. Make it quick, though. We're on a tight schedule, as you know.'

Lucius was astonished by this change of mind by Crassus. He'd never known him to grant favours to gladiators, however high-ranking. Was the famously tough lanista going soft?

Hector grinned and replaced his helmet. Meanwhile, Crassus walked over to Quin and whispered a few words to him. Quin nodded. Then Crassus moved off to the side, taking a seat near Lucius.

The Secutor was a heavily armed gladiator. He wore a full-face helmet with just two small eye holes, a large shield and a gladius. The Retiarius was lightly armoured, with no helmet, and he was armed with a weighted net, a trident and a dagger. Both gladiators' practice weapons were made of wood and weighted with iron, so they had the feel of real weapons without being life-threatening. The two began to circle each other. Quin held his trident two-handed, tilting it up towards Hector's head. Hector darted in swiftly, swinging his sword with violent intent towards Quin's chest. Quin leapt backwards and parried with his trident.

Lucius had watched enough of these fights to know that the Retiarius had to keep his distance to survive. Close-quarters fighting, where a gladius could be used to good effect, favoured the Secutor. So the Secutor, or Pursuer, was always trying to close in on the Retiarius, and the Retiarius was always backing off, waiting for an opportunity to stab the Secutor behind his shield with his long trident, or to throw his net. The longer the fight went on, the more exhausted the heavily armoured Secutor would become and the more likely a Retiarius victory. But Crassus had demanded a quick fight, which obviously favoured Hector.

The big Secutor was wasting no time going in for the kill. Since exhaustion was not going to be an issue, he was happy to use up all his energy in one sustained burst. He advanced on Quin with his upper body swaying, his arms swirling and his sword a blur. Hector's supporters yelled him on enthusiastically, and a smile flickered across Crassus's granite features.

It was hard to see how Quin managed to avoid this haze of deadly bladework, which seemed to dance so close to his arms, face and torso. But Quin's eyes had lost none of their hawklike focus, and his body, none of its catlike speed and agility. He flitted just beyond the boundaries of Hector's sword arcs with such uncanny precision, it was almost as if he knew where his opponent was going to strike next. If Hector's face could have been visible then, Lucius was sure it would show frustration and rage at this opponent who would never remain in one place long enough for him to land a blow. Quin's trident prongs or shaft were always in just the right place to block or parry. He made a block to the right knee, and, an impossibly short time later, he parried a blow to the left shoulder, quickly succeeded by a block to his right hip. And so it went on.

The cries of support for the primus palus diminished in volume and took on a slightly worried tone. Then, out of the blue, Quin struck. Twirling his trident so that the shaft end was now at the front, he landed a sharp and shocking blow to Hector's unshielded flank. The Secutor grunted in pained surprise. His fans gasped. Crassus frowned. Before Hector could recover, Quin jabbed the sharp end of the trident into his foot. The blunt wooden prong that struck just above the toes couldn't have penetrated far, but undoubtedly hurt a great deal, because Hector emitted a howl that must have been audible right across the quad. Another swift strike of the trident shaft to Hector's forearm knocked the gladius from his grip.

Lucius clenched his fists in suppressed triumph. Crassus had his head in his hands, not wishing to watch any more.

'Now use your net,' Lucius urged under his breath.

Quin unleashed the net in an underarm flick of the wrist. It draped itself over Hector's helmet and right shoulder – but it was a surprisingly weak and half-hearted throw, and the net simply slid away. It hung limply from Quin's wrist with all the menace of an onion bag. Hector looked up, astonished that Quin had fluffed his coup de grâce. He bent to pick up his sword, but Quin kicked it away.

And then a very strange thing happened: Quin picked up the heavy wooden gladius and struck himself hard across the face with its flat side. He staggered back a few paces, his cheek burning red from the blow. He stumbled onto his net and pulled the drawstring with a sharp tug, tripping himself up. Quin made a theatrical backward topple into the dust, his feet hopelessly entangled in the mesh. He looked up at the now totally bemused Hector and said: 'You win, sir. You have beaten me. You are the best here. Fact! You are the best there's ever been and ever likely to be. Fact! Now, if you don't mind, I would like to get back to my training.'

Silence reigned in the little amphitheatre as Quin disengaged himself from his net, rose to his feet and departed. Lucius got up and ran to join him. As he was leaving the arena, he heard the start of what sounded like a half-stifled fit of the giggles coming from one of Hector's supporters.

'What did Crassus say to you before the fight?' Lucius wanted to know, once he'd caught Quin up.

'He told me to lose.'

'Why would he do that?'

Quin shrugged. 'I have no idea.'

'Crassus must have realised you could beat Hector. Why do you think he's protecting him?'

'Search me,' said Quin. 'Maybe he's worried about morale. I guess it's not a good idea to make a fool of the primus palus just before the Roman Games.'

'But that's exactly what you ended up doing.' Lucius couldn't help smiling at the memory. 'You should have seen Crassus's face at the end.'

'I needed to teach that arrogant numbskull a lesson.'

'I think there's more to this, though,' frowned Lucius. 'There's something sinister going on. Hector's definitely got some sort of power over our lanista. As soon as Crassus saw it was him fighting, his whole attitude changed. He bent over backwards to please him – which is not like Crassus at all!'

CHAPTER VI

5 SEPTEMBER

On the morning of the opening day of the games, the dining hall was packed, as usual, with hungry gladiators gobbling down their breakfast. For those scheduled to fight that day, this was possibly their last full meal. Although the gladiators weren't due on until the afternoon, most would be too nervous to eat much come midday. Tensions were running high in the room. Arguments broke out easily, as tempers frayed and snapped. One young Murmillo* nearly broke the arm of a Hoplomachus just for spilling his water.

---

* *Murmillo: a gladiator who wears a distinctive crested helmet.*

A veteran Provocator punched a Thraex* on the nose because he had looked at him 'in a funny way'.

For Lucius, who was among those due to fight that afternoon, it really did seem like the last day. He sat alone, at the far end of one of the tables, and toyed with his barley broth. His dream of a last-minute intervention by Gaius or Isi had evaporated. It wasn't going to happen, and now he had to face the fact that he was doomed. According to the terms of his sentence, he was being sent into the arena without shield or armour of any kind. He had to fight a fully armed opponent dressed in nothing but a loincloth. He'd been working hard with Quin on developing his speed and dexterity of movement, but however fast he was, he knew he could never get close enough to his adversary to use his sword without exposing himself to lethal injury.

Quin came into the dining room now, surrounded by the usual cloud of friends and hangers-on. Ever since his humiliation of Hector in the training arena eleven days earlier, Quin had become one of the stars of the ludus, with about half of the auctorati, as well as most of the lower-class gladiators, happy to bask in his reflected glory. Quin disengaged himself from his entourage and came up to Lucius.

'Has Crassus told you who you're fighting yet?' he asked.

---

* *Thraex: a gladiator dressed as a Thracian (the Thracians were a warlike people from eastern Europe).*

Lucius shook his head. 'He's said nothing.'

Quin didn't seem surprised. Crassus had barely spoken to either of them since the incident with Hector.

'As far as Crassus is concerned, we're just criminals condemned to death,' said Lucius, chewing morosely on his barley. 'We might as well be damnati ad bestias.* It comes to the same thing.'

'Yeah, well you and I know different,' said Quin. 'So long as you have a sword in your hand, you always have a chance, right?'

This had been Quin's mantra since the beginning: *So long as you have a sword in your hand, you always have a chance*. It had sustained them through the weeks leading up to today. But now that the day had arrived, Lucius was forced to acknowledge how futile this hope really was.

'Remember to stay light on your feet, bro,' Quin continued. 'Keep moving about, and watch out for those tells. Check out his footwork, his sword positions, his breathing. There are always opportunities against any fighter, once you've worked out their style.'

A young Retiarius tapped Quin on the shoulder. 'Quintus, your breakfast has been served. Now will you come and sit with us?'

Quin's bright, hopeful blue eyes didn't leave Lucius's face. 'Just keep moving, and keep believing,' he said. 'Do you want to come and join us?'

* *damnati ad bestias: condemned to the wild beasts. Convicted criminals were devoured by beasts in the arena for the entertainment of the audience.*

121

Lucius attempted a smile. 'No thanks, I'll be OK.'

After giving him a final reassuring squeeze of the shoulder, Quin left and joined his friends.

Lucius sipped half-heartedly at the watery broth. His stomach had tightened as it always did when he was scared, and he felt numb inside. Even if the food had been full of flavour, he doubted he'd have been able to taste anything. All around him, the squabbles and bickering continued. It seemed that no one was in a good mood.

'Are you fighting today, Lucius?' asked a friendly voice. Lucius looked up. It was Sergius, who was now clambering onto the bench beside him.

'Yes,' he replied curtly, not being in a conversational mood.

'Good luck!' said Sergius.

The young tiro slurped some broth and said no more for a while, seemingly content to sit in companionable silence.

Eventually, Sergius looked up and said: 'I realise you'll probably die today…'

'Yup!' Lucius carried on scraping at the last dregs in his bowl, wondering why Sergius was even bothering to speak to him. He certainly wasn't cheering him up.

'…so I should probably tell you something,' Sergius continued.

'What's that?'

'You were my inspiration.'

Lucius looked at him. He had a pleasant, open face

with brown skin and a mop of curly black hair.

'What do you mean?' asked Lucius.

'I was in the crowd that day back in April when you defeated the tall Murmillo. What was his name again?'

'Eprius.'

'That was it! I was so impressed with your style, I decided to volunteer as a gladiator myself.' He chuckled. 'To be honest, it wasn't that hard a decision. See, I'd run away from home. My father is a drunk who regularly beat up my mother and me. I found myself a place to live: a tiny little room not far from here. No one in the ludus knew I was there. I stole food from the kitchens, and I could sneak into the amphitheatre whenever I wanted without a ticket. I got to see every show. But my life was empty. I needed a purpose, and the day I saw you, I found one. So, here I am, four months on, a tiro Laquearius,* about to have my first fight. And it was all down to you.'

Lucius snorted. 'I don't know if I should feel very proud about that. It's not much of a life.'

'You're wrong,' declared Sergius. 'It's everything I'd hoped for and more. For the first time in my life, I'm part of a familia. This ludus feels so much more like home than my actual home ever did.'

'I'm pleased for you,' said Lucius stiffly. At another time in his life, he would have welcomed Sergius as a friend. The boy seemed warm-hearted and decent. But right now, he couldn't see that there was any point.

* *Laquearius: a fighter with dagger and lasso.*

'I want to thank you for showing me my true path in life,' said Sergius. 'I know it's not much consolation at this time, but –'

He didn't manage to complete the sentence, for at that moment their attention was diverted by a cry of hysterical rage from one of the other tables.

'I'm not going to take it any longer!' someone bellowed. 'I refuse to accept this... this rat vomit... this stinking broth of Hades, which tastes and smells like the inside of a legionary's loincloth after a fifteen-hour march! By all the gods, it's the morning of the opening of the Roman Games! I demand fresh fruit!'

Lucius and Sergius were not entirely surprised to see that the source of this protest was Hilario, who had always been the most vocal critic of the food served up at the ludus. He was standing up, his eyebrows at a fierce angle, spittle flecking the sides of his mouth. Perhaps it was the tension of the day, but something must have finally snapped inside him, because after delivering this speech, he picked up his bowl and threw it over the slave who had handed it to him, covering the poor lad in warm, greasy water, bits of barley and chopped carrots.

Two guards strode up to Hilario and shoved him back onto his bench, but Hilario immediately rose again and began throwing punches at them. Suddenly, the whole dining hall was in uproar. Gladiators leapt to their feet and began hurling their own bowls of broth at the guards who were attacking Hilario, while others started shouting their support for the mutinous Provocator and bashing their bowls and spoons on the tables. The noise was deafening. It was as if Hilario's outburst had cut the rope on a ballista,* unleashing all the anger and tension that had been building up over the past weeks and months. More guards poured into the room and began battering the rioting gladiators with wooden staves. The gladiators retaliated by bashing the guards with their fists, bowls and spoons.

Lucius was astonished at how quickly a normal breakfast scene could descend into complete chaos, and maybe even rebellion. Everyone seemed to be joining in. He saw Quin in the midst of it all, diving off a table onto three guards, pushing them to the floor. Something stirred inside Lucius – a flicker of hope? Maybe, if they could work together, they could break out of this place, escape to the hills, and live to fight another day.

'This is wrong!' he heard Sergius whining. 'They'll destroy everything! We have to stop them.'

'No,' murmured Lucius, picking up his own bowl and spoon. 'This is right.' He launched himself into the mêlée.

All of the school's sixty gladiators were in the room, including forty-five slave- and criminal-class fighters, every one of whom joined in the fight against

---

* *ballista: a Roman artillery weapon, a giant crossbow powered by twisted skeins of animal sinew.*

the guards. They, after all, had least to lose and most to gain from a rebellion: they were fighting for their very lives and their freedom. But for the fifteen auctorati, the situation was slightly different. They had volunteered for this life, and although they might not like the food much, they didn't necessarily want to destroy the school. In the end, just four auctorati, including Hilario, rebelled, while another four stood quietly on the sidelines, and the remaining seven, led by Hector, joined the guards against the gladiators.

There were thirty guards. They wore helmets and armour and wielded heavy wooden clubs, and with the support of Hector and his friends, they seemed, at first, to be winning the battle of the dining hall, forcing the gladiators back towards the rear of the room. But then Hilario ordered the gladiators to overturn one of the long trestle tables, and this formed a barricade that served to hold back the advancing line of guards. At the same time, Quin led a raid on the kitchens and his team purloined dozens of heavy cooking pots and utensils. From behind their barricade, the gladiators proceeded to hurl these objects at the guards to devastating effect. They followed up this artillery barrage with a headlong stampede that reversed the course of the battle. The gladiators pushed back against their enemy, and within minutes, the last dazed and injured guard was ejected from the room. Hector, his friends, and the neutral auctorati – including Sergius – were also thrown out.

The remaining gladiators gave an almighty cheer, and Hilario and Quin were paraded around the room on the shoulders of their troops in an impromptu triumph. It was much too early to celebrate, of course – Lucius knew that. He tried desperately to warn the others that they should try and make their escape now, while the ludus was still in disarray. But no one seemed willing to listen. They were drunk on the ecstasy of victory, and happy to plunder the kitchens for the better-quality food served to the lanista and his coaching staff.

They were helping themselves to fistfuls of apples, grapes, figs and oranges when the Praetorians arrived. The clattering rhythm of the iron-soled sandals coming down the corridor sent a shudder of fear and despair through Lucius. The white-plumed elite troops charged into the dining hall and began pushing gladiators to the ground, pinning them there with swordpoints to their fruit-smeared faces. The rebels were outnumbered and out-armoured. Within minutes, the uprising was over.

Crassus appeared and walked among the clusters of restrained gladiators. His face was flushed almost purple, and his squat, muscular body quivered with fury. 'You've disgraced yourselves, all of you!' he bawled at them. 'You've brought shame upon the name of this ludus! Training is cancelled this morning. You will be confined to your dormitories under heavy guard until a suitable punishment can be devised. You will live to regret this moment of lunacy, I can promise you that!' He ordered the commander of the Praetorian troop to take them away.

'This isn't over,' Hilario hissed at Quin before they were led off in their separate directions. Lucius was impressed and encouraged by the defiance in the Provocator's expression, despite the blood streaming from his squashed nose.

'Too right,' Quin whispered back. 'This place is ready to explode. We showed that this morning.'

Training might have been cancelled, but of course the Roman Games couldn't be. Early that afternoon, the gladiators who were due to fight were ushered from their rooms and escorted along an underground tunnel that led from the ludus to the hypogeum – the basement of the Flavian Amphitheatre – a short distance to the west. Among them was Lucius, who was in the first scheduled fight of the games. The dining-hall uprising had come too late to save him. Still, he hoped it would prove the start of something bigger – a mass breakout, perhaps – that would allow Quin to save his own life.

From the hypogeum, he was led up some steps and shown into a little room beneath the stands where he was told to get kitted up. The thrusting spear was there on a table waiting for him, along with the gladius and dagger – but of course there was no helmet, shield or armour. The slave who brought Lucius his pre-fight drink of posca* was a small, wiry man with sharp eyes and a crooked smile. He told Lucius what he knew of his opponent. 'He's a tiro Thraex from the Ludus Dacius,** the slave said. 'Looks hyped up on nervous energy. I think the strategy is to break him in gently on a damnatus ad gladium. No offence, mate, but his trainer clearly believes that killing you will give the kid the extra confidence he needs to set himself up for a lengthy career.'

'Sounds like a good plan,' said Lucius grimly as he sipped his drink.

His stomach tightened as a deep horn blast cut through the excited hubbub of the crowd outside. That was the cue to make his way to the arena entrance. He sheathed the sword and dagger in his belt, picked up his spear and exited the room. At the far end of the corridor, standing at the arched entrance, was the Thraex he was due to fight. As the slave had described, the lad seemed very nervous, and this was betrayed by constant twitchy movements, from jerks of his head to an incessant shaking of his legs. The boy refused even to acknowledge Lucius as he drew up alongside him. His eyes darted from the ceiling to the floor, looking anywhere but towards the opponent on his left. This gave Lucius some encouragement. Perhaps

* posca: watered-down vinegar or soured wine, flavoured with herbs.
** Ludus Dacius: a specialist school on the Oppian Hill in Rome, where prisoners from the wars in Dacia (present-day Romania and Moldova) were trained to become Thracian gladiators.

he could use the boy's anxiety to his advantage. The tiro had everything to prove and everything to lose in this contest. As a condemned criminal expected to die, Lucius was unencumbered by any such expectations. In a curious way, he was much more free.

At another horn signal, they walked out side by side onto the sand. It was a blustery day with clouds flitting across the bright sky, making the white sand shimmer with light and shade like the bottom of a shallow sunlit sea. The swelling roar of the crowd was like waves crashing around them. Without helmet, shield, manica or greave, Lucius felt strangely naked, as if this was all a dream and he'd forgotten to put on his clothes.

His eyes flitted towards the banked seating that rose up around him like an oval canyon, studded with countless faces all staring in his direction. There were no bookies moving among them – no one was taking bets on this fight. Yet the crowd seemed excited anyway. Many of Quin's Suburran supporters were in attendance and they had quickly grasped that his brother was before them now, about to fight for his life. As Lucius walked towards the centre, they gave him a throaty cheer, to the evident disapproval of those in the patrician seats. For the senators and other wealthy Romans, the damnati ad gladium were the worst class of criminal and should be booed rather than applauded. Their death in the arena was just another form of execution, like crucifixion or being thrown to the lions.

But they could do nothing about the mob's perverse tendency to idolise such scoundrels, and when the summa rudis* mentioned Lucius's name, the spectators erupted into another enthusiastic roar. 'Lucius Valerius Aquila!' shouted the summa rudis. He continued above the thunderous cheering: 'convicted of patricide and other foul deeds! Damnatus ad gladium – condemned to die by the sword in the arena! According to his sentence, he must fight without protection from helmet, shield or armour.'

After he had introduced the Thraex, whose name was Decebalus, to more moderate applause, the summa rudis called for the fight to begin. Decebalus donned his griffin-crested helmet and immediately came for Lucius, his curved sword slicing angular shapes in the air. The young tiro must have been advised to be aggressive from the outset. He had every opportunity for a quick victory, after all, with so much unprotected flesh within range.

Lucius backed off, but slowly, as Quin had recommended. His brother's words echoed in his head: *Bait him... make him think he's got you...* Decebalus was closing in now, coming within range of Lucius's flesh. The timing had to be perfect. Just as Decebalus's sword began descending towards his neck, Lucius leapt swiftly to his left and thrust his spear at Decebalus's exposed shoulder. But the Dacian was quicker than Lucius had expected. He dipped into a crouch, and

* *summa rudis: senior referee.*

131

Lucius's spear bounced harmlessly off the top of his helmet.

Decebalus brought his sword round in a flat arc, parallel to the ground, towards Lucius's unprotected shin. Lucius jumped, bringing his knees up as high as he could. The blade hissed close enough to shave his leg hairs. When his feet touched sand again, he quickly spun away. *Round One to Decebalus*, Lucius had to admit. The boy hadn't fallen for his ambush, and had almost inflicted a surprise of his own. Perhaps he wasn't as nervous as he looked.

Lucius switched his spear to his left hand and drew out his sword just in time to parry a strike towards his face. He tried to go on the attack, but Decebalus refused to yield ground, and for a while they hacked blade to blade, making sharp ringing sounds that echoed around the amphitheatre.

Stalemate!

But Lucius could never relax his focus even fractionally, knowing that a single missed parry would be enough to bring death or dismemberment. His sword had to be everywhere – it was his weapon and also his shield. He tried to fall in with the rhythm of his opponent, as Quin had taught him – tried to get inside his mind and his thoughts, so that nothing could surprise him. It was easier said than done. Out here in the heat and sweat of battle, he felt as though he was floundering, lurching from one defensive posture to the next without really knowing what he was doing, and every snatched breath felt like his last. His opponent seemed to be gaining in strength and energy. Each vicious sword strike sent painful vibrations shooting through Lucius's arm, and sparks flying off his blade.

Lucius was tiring, his feet heavy as they dragged through the sand. He knew he couldn't keep moving his sword at the same pace for much longer. Sooner or later, one of these attacks would break through his defences and rip into his flesh. He had to do something – anything – to unnerve Decebalus. He jabbed his spear at him, but it rebounded harmlessly off his circular shield. He tried again, higher. The spear struck the Dacian's manica but he barely seemed to notice. Lucius was being forced back. He no longer had the energy for counterstrikes, only blocks. He fended off a strike that would have taken off his nose and then another that would have removed his leg at the knee. The crowd were making nightmarish sounds – groaning and howling. Lucius had heard these sorts of animal noises before, in the endgame of previous fights he'd witnessed, when they smelled blood in the air. This time it was *his* blood they smelled. Well, he would make them wait a little longer. He fought on, pushing his muscles beyond all previous endurance levels. Pain arrowed through his arm and shoulder with every movement. His knees were buckling. The sweat was pouring off him.

Decebalus was relentless. He slashed at Lucius, who raised his sword in defence, but the handle slipped in the grease coating his palm. The sword fell from his grasp and spun into the sand. Decebalus, seeing the opening, darted forward and slashed again. Lucius felt a horrible slicing in his chest and saw the blood-gleam on the tip of his opponent's curved blade. He felt himself slowing, life and energy seeping out of him. There was hardly any pain. He went down on his knees as the sun emerged from cloud, bathing him in light. From somewhere came the sound of laughter and splashes. He could feel Isi's breath against his cheek. Then something flashed above him like a metal raptor diving for the kill. He raised his spear to block. There was a loud crack and the spear shaft shattered. The force of the blow sent Lucius sprawling onto his back. Decebalus's blade had missed his hand by a skin's thickness. Not even that – for blood, he now saw, was spilling from the base of his thumb.

Lucius felt the thunder of his heartbeat in his ears. Then the pain from his chest arrived. It rose up in waves from his wound, knifing through the fog in his head. He needed some time, but the world and Decebalus wouldn't wait. He could sense the blade coming back for him, greedy for more of his flesh. He twisted away from it, feeling the sand encrust itself in the wound on his chest. His hands flapped at the pale dust, seeking purchase so he could rise. His fingers scraped against something hard and sharp, half-buried in the sand.

Above him, the sun dazzled. The silhouette of a

helmeted figure moved across it, sword raised high. Decebalus was closing in for the kill. A memory flashed into Lucius's brain just then, of watching Quin training with the leopard in the Morning School, marvelling at the way that subtle predator had moved with inhuman speed, using the natural springiness and flexibility in its spine. He recalled one time when the wounded leopard had lain on its side, barely breathing, and as Quin approached, it had suddenly leapt up and, with a slash of its paw, had nearly broken Quin's neck. In the days of their incarceration, the brothers had devised exercises for themselves, hoping that some of this 'cat motion', as Quin called it, might just make up for their lack of armour in the arena. Each morning in their cell, before breakfast, they had practised these moves – swaying, dodging, twisting, turning, leaping. Quin was superior to Lucius in all but one of these exercises…

Decebalus twirled the sword in his hands so that it was pointing downwards. With the handle clamped between both his fists, he drove it hard into Lucius's heaving stomach.

But Lucius was no longer there. The sword tip embedded itself in sand.

For some reason, Lucius had always been quicker than his brother at the 'playing dead' trick: lying on his back and then springing to his feet.

While Decebalus was still pulling his blade from the sand, Lucius took a flying kick at his leg, toppling him.

By the time Decebalus had recovered his senses, he could see the tip of Lucius's sword pointing at his throat.

But adrenaline could carry Lucius only so far. A wave of dizziness swept over him and he began to stagger. Forcing himself to remain conscious, he let himself sink to his knees while keeping the tip of his blade firmly in place below the Dacian's Adam's apple. Decebalus raised a finger in surrender. It took a few seconds for the crowd to take in what had happened, but soon enough the roars of shock, surprise and elation began to detonate like a series of explosions right across the upper tier of the amphitheatre. From the patrician seats, closer to the arena, barely any sound could be heard.

Lucius could feel the blood slick against his skin as far down as his loincloth. The wound felt like a raw, gaping cavern in his chest. He couldn't bring himself to look at it, fearing he might see his own ribs and heart. He was helped to his feet by an official, and found enough strength to raise his arm in acknowledgement of his supporters. Then he collapsed and everything went dark.

CHAPTER VII

5–6 SEPTEMBER

When his eyes opened again, it was to glimpse, as if through a watery haze, the face of Aelius Eumenes gazing down on him. He blinked, and his sight cleared. He felt weak and muzzy-headed. Pain throbbed in his chest but no longer with such urgency. It felt cooler there, benumbed. Eumenes must have used one of his amazing pain-relieving ointments.

'How am I doing, Doctor?' he croaked.

'You'll be fine,' said Eumenes unsmilingly. 'The wound is superficial. No major damage done.'

Relief was like sweet honey in his veins. It had felt like a mortal wound at the time. He'd been lucky. Glancing down, he saw his chest swathed in a clean, white linen bandage. 'Thank you,' he gasped, and he wondered why Eumenes's expression remained grim.

'You lost quite a bit of blood,' the doctor said. 'If Crassus allows it, I'd advise you take a long rest.'

'If Crassus allows it?'

'Officially you're under sentence of death,' said Eumenes. 'The rules aren't clear about what to do if a damnatus gets injured during a fight – whether he should be sent back out there so that someone else can finish the job, or be allowed to recover from his wounds first. It's left up to individual lanistae to make a judgement on that. I know that Crassus likes you, so you may be given a reprieve. On the other hand, he's been in a stinking mood since your little mutiny this morning, so who knows what he'll decide. In the meantime I've been told to return you to your cell. All gladiators not actually fighting or undergoing surgery must be locked in their cells at all times. Those are the new rules.'

Slaves were summoned and Lucius was transported back to his cell on a stretcher. Quin immediately rose from his straw bed when Lucius entered. After the slaves had gone and the guard had closed and relocked the door, Quin greeted Lucius with a bear hug that made him wince.

'Careful, brother!' he hissed.

'Sorry! I'm just so relieved you survived. You did it, Lu! Was it the "cat motion"?'

Lucius nodded. 'I played dead, like your leopard.'

His grin was partly a rictus of pain. 'You should have seen me, Quin. I was so quick. The Dacian didn't know what hit him.'

'That's my boy!' said Quin, clapping him, more gently this time, on the shoulder. Then he frowned. 'How bad is that wound?'

'It'll be OK. Eumenes says it just needs time. But I may not be given that. Crassus is apparently within his rights to send me straight back out there.'

'With any luck, he won't get the chance,' said Quin.

'What do you mean?'

Lucius was excited by the dramatic gleam in his brother's eyes. What had happened?

'There have been developments,' said Quin. 'As you know, this ludus is like a flaming arrow at the moment, just waiting for someone to fire it. Well, Hilario and I are going to fire the arrow tonight.'

Lucius's eyes bulged with surprise. This sounded utterly reckless, even by Quin's standards. 'Tonight? But the guards will be on full alert, and the place is probably still crawling with Praetorians. We couldn't possibly break out of here. How are we even going to get out of our cells?'

'We're going to get some outside help.'

'From who?'

'Isi.'

Lucius could only stare at his brother in open-mouthed bewilderment. *How could Isi be playing a role in all this?*

139

'I found a little note stuck to the back of the spoon that arrived with my barley broth,' explained Quin. '"From a friend of Isidora," it read. "There will be no guards at the main door at the start of the third watch tonight.* Riots in Suburra at the same time."'

'It must have come from Durio, the head porter,' muttered Lucius. 'He's always had a soft spot for Isi. Calls her his "Nile Princess".'

Quin laughed. 'Good old Isi, eh? I knew she'd come through for us. And I guess she must have arranged with her gangster friends in Suburra to start a little uprising of their own, which will keep the main force of Praetorians occupied while we make our escape.'

'But how are we going to get out of our cells?'

'That's where Sergius comes in.'

'Sergius?'

Lucius was plunged back into confusion. He remembered how distressed the mop-headed young Laquearius had been when the fighting broke out that morning, and how he'd eventually been ejected from the dining hall by the rebel gladiators, along with all the other loyalist auctorati. When he reminded Quin of this, a cynical yet indulgent smile formed on his brother's lips.

'Sergius is an innocent, I agree. He actually believes there's honour in the gladiator game, as I once did. He loves the whole idea of the familia because he never had a family of his own. But Sergius is also a friend.

* third watch: about 3.00 a.m.

It didn't take him long to come to his senses. Soon after I got that message from Durio, he paid me a visit – he's still allowed the run of the place, as one of the few who stayed loyal. I told him about the note I got, and he immediately offered to spread the word among the other rebel leaders. When the bell rings to signal the start of the third watch, that'll be our cue to start raising a rumpus. With all the dormitories in uproar, the guards will start to panic. Sergius will jump the guard on Hilario's cell – he's one of the weedier-looking ones, apparently. Once Hilario and his mates are freed from their cell, there'll be enough of them to overpower the guards in their corridor. Sergius swears he'll be along here as soon as he can to free us so we can join the escape.'

Lucius gave a tight smile. He was happy and excited, of course he was. But it was all a bit too soon for him. 'I'm afraid I'll slow you down,' he said. 'You're best off escaping on your own.'

'Not a chance,' said Quin. 'You're coming with me, Lu, even if I have to carry you.'

During the following hours, Lucius tried to relax as much as possible, but it was difficult with Quin almost crackling with nervous energy. When he wasn't restlessly pacing the floor, he was doing chin-ups on the beam from which the oil lamp hung. And when he was done with those, he went through his cat motions again and again, until his body became a blur and Lucius grew dizzy from looking at him.

'Give it a rest, Quin,' he pleaded. 'Or you'll have no strength left for tonight.'

Quin took a break, hands on knees, waiting for his breath to return. His tunic was dark with sweat. 'Whenever... I'm excited about anything... I have to exercise,' he panted.

Lucius loved his brother but, not for the first time, he wished they had separate rooms.

They measured time by meals and by the degree of light penetrating their cell from the tiny, barred window above Lucius's bed. Their evening meal was delivered after sunset, during the first watch of the night. They ate the broth in tense silence. After the meal, Quin resumed his pacing.

'It's late,' said Lucius. 'Get some sleep or you'll regret it later. I promise I'll wake you when the time comes.'

Reluctantly, Quin settled down on his bed. He lay there staring up at the low ceiling, fingers nervously drumming against the stone floor. Lucius gazed up from his bed at a cobweb that ornamented the angle of wall and beam, its dusty threads wafting in the night breeze from the window. Gradually, he felt his eyes start to close.

He never heard the bell. Luckily, Quin did, and Lucius was awoken by the noise of his brother stomping about the room, bashing his spoon against his empty bowl. When the pottery receptacle shattered, he began battering the spoon against the door and rattling it on the iron grille. Echoes of equally rowdy noisemaking drifted up the corridor from other parts of the ludus.

The rebellion was on!

The guard outside their door bellowed a fierce warning: 'Stop that now or I'll come in there and rip your arms off!'

Quin ignored the threat and banged his spoon even more forcefully. Lucius sat up and grabbed his own bowl and spoon to add to the din. The vigorous movements of his arm sent ripples of pain through his chest, but he didn't stop. He hoped the guards would take fright at this simultaneous attack of noise from all sides, even though the gladiators were still safely imprisoned behind their locked doors. Not for long, though – Sergius should be seeing to that problem right now. Lucius trembled with excitement. He prayed his wound wouldn't slow him down when the time came to make their escape. He didn't want Quin to be delayed by him and risk recapture. He'd much sooner stay here if it improved his brother's chances, but convincing Quin of that would be difficult.

The cell guard continued to shout his threats and curses at them, but he didn't follow them up, probably fearing that he would be ambushed as soon as he set foot through the door. The noises from other parts of the ludus soon changed from shouts and spoon-bashing to something much more violent and extreme. Screams echoed up the stone corridors along with groans of pain and the thud of fists and iron soles being driven into bodies. This was accompanied by the heavy clatter of running footsteps, panicked shouts, banging doors and the frenzied clanging of the emergency bell.

'It's happening!' cried Quin. 'Any moment now, Sergius or Hilario'll be here and they'll let us out.'

The noise of the battle continued, but no running footsteps could be heard coming in their direction, and no scuffle with the guard outside their door. The longer this went on, the more Quin's triumphant smile staled and became a grimace of frustration. Eventually, they heard a barked instruction from somewhere nearby and the sound of their guard running away, presumably to help out his comrades.

Quin cursed and banged his fist against the door. 'What happened to them?' he cried. 'They were supposed to come here first and let us out! Now the guard's gone off and taken the cell keys with him!' He roared through the grille: 'Sergius! Hilario! Where are you?!'

'They knew I'd slow you guys down,' said Lucius quietly. 'They took a decision...'

'No!' screamed Quin, turning on Lucius in a rage. 'They'd never do that! I know them. They're good men, both of them.' He turned back to the door and kicked it viciously. 'They must have come unstuck. Maybe this sector is too heavily guarded.'

Lucius and Quin could only listen in growing exasperation to the cheers of the gladiators as they gradually overpowered the guards. The noise of the fight began to fade as the rebels made their way towards the now unguarded main entrance.

'I can't believe it,' gasped Quin, despair almost robbing him of breath. He sat down heavily on his bed and put his head in his hands.

Lucius didn't know what to say. He still wasn't sure he'd have made it, even if things had gone according to plan. Even so, he felt desperate. To continue their fight against Glabrio, Quin, at least, had to get out of here, and now that wasn't going to happen. Isi would be crushed when they didn't emerge, but there was nothing she or anyone could do about it. From tomorrow, security would be doubled, trebled, on the ludus – assuming they weren't immediately executed on a charge of aiding and abetting the mass breakout.

He lay back on his bed. The cobweb above his head seemed to mock him, with its dusty bags of silk reflecting moonlight and floating in a breeze from another world – a world of freedom that he would never experience again.

And then, as he lay there, something small and dark tore across his vision and ripped through the heart of the web, blowing it into powdery filaments that trembled and shrank to nothing. The small, dark something landed with a soft thump next to Lucius's head. Instinctively he grabbed it and then had to cling on tight as it nearly jerked out of his grasp. The thing was heavy and rough to the touch like... like the knotted end of a rope! Glancing up, Lucius saw that the rope was dangling down from between the bars of the little window. He felt himself rising, being hauled to his feet by whatever was pulling at the other end. His chest was in agony as his muscles tightened around the edges of his wound. On tiptoes, he tried to peer through the window, but it was too high up to show anything but a patch of starlit sky.

The rope was being pulled by something of quite unbelievable strength, and it felt to Lucius as though his chest was being ripped apart with the effort of holding on. He could almost hear the stitches bursting down there. Yet he knew somehow that he mustn't let go. This was their chance. Whatever unearthly agent had sent this rope end flying into their cell, its object must have been to break them out of here, and it wouldn't be able to do that unless he held on.

But the pain was just too great. The rope began to slide through his hands, burning the skin of his palms. At the last moment he heard a cry from the other side of the cell, and suddenly Quin was by his side, his strong fists closing over the rope, stopping it. With a roar of effort, Quin pulled at the rope and managed, briefly, to reverse its progress away from them, forcing a short length of it back through the window. Hurriedly,

Quin wound the end of the rope around one of the window's iron bars and knotted it. Then he tied a second knot for good measure before falling back from the window. Lucius clutched his chest and felt warm wetness soaking through his tunic. He sighed and bit his lip against the pain. *He would get through this!*

They both watched as the rope tautened against the iron bar. It creaked as the pressure mounted. At one point Lucius was sure that the double knot would unravel – but it held. Cracks began to spider the wall surrounding the window and Lucius could only wonder what godlike power was at work here. What strength could threaten the very fabric of a building as solidly made as the Ludus Romanus?

The rope thinned to the point where it looked about to snap, the iron bar began to bend, and the tracery of cracks became ever wider and deeper. Soon the cracks began to link up to form a single, roughly circular fracture in the brickwork, about five feet in diameter. Quin began launching flying kicks at the bricks inside the circle, helping to weaken the crumbling area of wall still further. Lucius would certainly have joined in if he'd been able to.

Finally, with a great grinding and cracking and an eruption of brick dust, the window and a large chunk of its surrounding wall was ripped free and tumbled with a deafening crash to the ground below. Coughing and choking, Lucius and Quin squinted through the gaping hole in their cell wall to see what was out there.

PART THREE

FUGITIVES

CHAPTER VIII

6 SEPTEMBER

s the dust cleared, they found themselves looking out into the broad street that ran alongside the ludus. Towering above them in the middle of the street, no more than ten paces away, was a huge, grey, wrinkled shape with a long, thin appendage dangling from its middle, supported by legs the thickness of tree trunks. It took Lucius no more than a few seconds to identify the shape as the rear view of an elephant, and not just any elephant – from the deep scar to her flank, he knew it to be Magnentia, his old friend from his days working at the vivarium. Two long ropes hung from a harness attached to Magnentia's shoulders and belly, and these had been joined to form the single rope that

had been dropped through their window and was still attached to the mess of iron bars and brickwork that lay smashed in the street in front of them.

Towards the front end of Magnentia, just behind her head, was a saddle supporting a small figure, who had turned around to look at them. With a rush of joy, Lucius recognised the figure as their sister Valeria. The last time he'd seen her was more than four months ago, at the Temple of Venus Genetrix, and once again he was struck by her beauty and the shadows of sadness around her eyes. Yet her evident delight at seeing her brothers seemed to dispel a lot of that sadness. Laughing, she slid off the saddle, jumped lightly to the ground and ran to them. Quin reached her first. He swept her off her feet and spun her around before smothering her with kisses.

'My dear, sweet sister!' he cried. 'How tall and beautiful you've become!'

'Ssshh!' she hushed him, her face still one huge smile. 'We must be quiet.' They were hardly likely to be overheard, though, above the clamour of fighting at the front of the ludus.

As Lucius hobbled out onto the street, his attention was immediately redirected to his right. At the far end lay the wide, well-lit concourse that separated the ludus from the Flavian Amphitheatre, and this was the scene of a fierce battle between the escaping gladiators and a cohort* of the Praetorian Guard.

* *cohort: a unit of about 480 men. Ten cohorts make a legion.*

Evidently, Isi's uprising in Suburra hadn't provided enough of a diversion.

He hardly had time to take this in before he felt Val's hot, sweet breath against his cheek and her arms clamping themselves around his waist. 'Oh, Lu!' she sighed. 'I've missed you so much!'

He gasped with pain. 'Val! Please!' He detached himself from her, clutching his wound.

'Oh!' she whispered, horrified. 'You're hurt! I'm so sorry!'

'It's OK,' he breathed. 'Nothing serious. It's so great to see you.'

A boy emerged hesitantly from the trunk end of Magnentia. He was carrying an ankus, a stick used to guide and control elephants.

Val turned to him. 'Thank you for everything, Gajadhar,' she said. 'Lead her back to the gardens now. And be quiet! I don't want Mother or the master to know what you and Magnentia did for me tonight.'

'You are not coming back then, Mistress?' said Gajadhar. He looked sad.

'No,' she said, with a glance at Lucius and Quin. 'I never want to go back.'

Magnentia nuzzled Lucius, remembering his smell. He patted her tenderly on the trunk. 'I owe you one, big girl,' he murmured.

They watched as Gajadhar detached the ropes from her harness and led Magnentia away. It was beyond strange, seeing this enormous animal striding through

the moonlight down an ordinary street in the middle of
Rome. Lucius wondered if anything could surprise him
again after the events of this night. He turned to Val,
bursting with questions about how she had managed
to bring off this amazing rescue, but before he could
ask any of them, the air was filled with the clatter of
approaching footsteps. His heart skipped several beats.
If the guards or the Praetorians came for them now, he
didn't think he'd be capable of running. But to his great
relief, the figures that emerged from the shadows were
familiar and friendly: Isi and her old friend Faustina,
with Sergius and Hilario. Surprisingly, bringing up
the rear was Hector, the primus palus. What was *he*
doing here? Lucius had assumed he would be fighting
on the side of the guards and the Praetorians against
the rebel gladiators.

Once again, though, he was denied any chance to
ask questions. Isi hugged him gently, mindful of his
wound. But as he opened his mouth to speak, she
put a finger to his lips and beckoned him to follow.
Then she led him and the others at a fast pace down
the street, away from the battle on the concourse and
into a dingy side alley. Lucius, towards the rear of the
group, hobbled along as fast as he could, every footstep
sending a stab of pain through his chest. As they ran
along the dim, narrow backstreet, his ears were assailed
by the snores of beggars and the mewling of cats.
He smelled rotting vegetables and stale wine and
once or twice felt his feet slide into some soft,

foul-smelling residue. At one point they passed close to the marble colonnade of the Temple of Claudius – a glimpse of opulence amid the general squalor. A short while later, they passed beneath a towering red arch of the Anio Novus aqueduct, striding its way grandly towards the hilltop mansions of the Palatine.

From these clues, Lucius calculated that they were heading southwest. This puzzled him, as it was taking them deeper into the heart of the city when surely they ought to be trying to get out of Rome. But with the pain in his chest and the effort of keeping up with the others, Lucius found he had no energy left to query Isi's choice of direction.

Finally, they emerged into the broad thoroughfare of the Via Appia. Torches hung from the pillars of arches, casting a smudgy golden glow on the black cobbles. To their left was the enormous sweeping frontage of Rome's chariot-racing arena, the Circus Maximus. Straight ahead was the southeastern corner of the Palatine Hill, dominated by the old palace of the Julio-Claudian emperors. Virtually destroyed in the Great Fire,* it was now a beautiful, crumbling ruin, its moon-washed marble façade peeping out from behind a forest of cypress trees.

The Palatine was also home to the richest and most powerful people in Rome – including Glabrio. 'So you

---

* *Great Fire: the Great Fire of Rome occurred in AD 64, during the reign of the emperor Nero. It began on 16 July and raged for six days. Nero's enemies later claimed that he had started the fire himself.*

brought us here!' said Quin angrily. 'Right under the noses of our enemies! Wise move!'

Isi hushed him with a finger, and signalled them to follow her down the Vicus Consinius, which ran between the Circus Maximus and the southern side of the Palatine. Lucius took a deep breath, bracing himself for another bout of painful motion, and hobbled after her. They ran along the ruler-straight street for some two hundred paces, past the endless colonnade of the racetrack on their left and a row of tenement buildings on their right. Lucius couldn't imagine what it would be like to live in one of these apartments on race days, when the noise must be overwhelming. Above the tenements could be glimpsed, in occasional gaps between the trees, the towering columns and courtyards of the old palace.

The tenements eventually gave way to a fenced-off area. Isi led them through a gap in the fence onto a disused piece of land on the steeply sloping flank of the Palatine. The place was wild with overgrown vegetation, and in the moonlight it seemed an exotic jungle, like those described by traders who'd visited the faraway land of India. There were giant ferns the size of small trees, and the ground was entirely cloaked in green leaves through which moss-covered boulders peeped. Almost hidden beneath the greenery, the foundation walls of the old palace could be seen rising up the hillside towards the magnificent ruins above. Thick-stemmed creepers pressed themselves into the cracked stonework, forming a tangled lattice that seemed to have conjoined with the ramparts to form a strange structure, part natural, part human-made.

They scrambled up the steep and slippery slope and then stopped in surprise as Isi seemed to disappear into the leaves and branches of a heavily drooping tree above their heads. Pushing their way up through the mass of fronds, they found no sign of her and wondered where she'd got to. Then Valeria spotted a crack in the palace wall through which the trunk of the tree had burst. It was narrow, dark and virtually invisible – until a soft, beckoning glow appeared there. Lucius waited as each member of the group passed through the crack. It was a tight fit, especially for Hector and Hilario, the biggest members of the group.

They found themselves in a damp-smelling subterranean passageway. Isi was waiting for them there, a lit torch in her hand. As soon as they were all safely through, she turned and began walking along the passage, heading deeper beneath the hill. Lucius, feeling weak and dizzy from pain after all the running, climbing and squeezing, limped along at the back of the group and prayed that they were near the end of their journey. The floor of the passage was uneven with stones that lay in wait to trip unwary feet. Lucius glimpsed slimy, rough-hewn walls and a vaulted ceiling from which water dripped echoingly.

After a few minutes of halting progress, the passage ended in a small wooden door. The door was lit by another torch, and it took Lucius a moment to see that this torch was actually being held by a small, elderly, bearded figure in a dirty cloak. It disturbed him to think that anyone could live in this cold, dark underground place.

'Thank you for meeting us here, Sacerdos,'* murmured Isi. 'Will you open the door for us?'

The priest nodded. In his other hand, he carried a large iron key on an iron hoop. He pushed the key into the door's rusty lock and twisted. The mechanism made a reluctant grinding sound and the door swung open on creaking hinges. Isi led them through the door and down a narrow set of stone steps. Lucius gasped in amazement as he caught flashes of beauty and riches revealed in the flickering glow of her torch. They were entering some sort of underground grotto. Its walls were encrusted with brilliantly coloured mosaics and seashells – thousands upon thousands of them glittered in the torchlight.

'What is this place?' gasped Sergius.

'The Lupercal,' answered a deep voice from above.

They all turned to see the little priest standing at the top of the steps glaring down at them, his head haloed by the torch in his hand. His face was pale, almost white, above his dark beard, his eyes a bestial yellow. Lucius's sense of wonder increased tenfold at the priest's words. The Lupercal was the legendary cave where the foundling twins Romulus and Remus

* *Sacerdos: priest.*

were suckled by a she-wolf. He had no idea that the location of the cave was even known – he had assumed until now that it was little more than myth.*

The priest continued: 'It was discovered by the emperor Augustus more than a century ago, when the foundations were being laid for the palace that lies directly above us. Augustus ordered it to be decorated as a sacred shrine, and appointed a priest to take care of it. That priest was my great-grandfather. The emperors that followed all worshipped here – until Nero. And the Great Fire that destroyed the palace during his reign also brought an end to the imperial visits to the Lupercal – for the only access, apart from your own route here tonight, was from the palace. The shrine is now all but forgotten by the outside world, but I continue to maintain it and make sacrifices here each February during the festival of Lupercalia, as my forefathers did before me. You are welcome to remain here for as long as you need to, my friends, but I beg you to show respect to this shrine as the nursing-place of our founding fathers.'

With that, the priest gave a small bow and departed.

Lucius allowed his weary body to collapse upon the cold stone floor, and he leaned back against the gentle curve at the base of the wall. The others followed suit, forming a rough circle. Faustina shared out some

---

* *little more than myth: in 2007, archaeologists discovered a highly decorated cave beneath the palace of the emperor Augustus. Some believe that this is the Lupercal, but others are not convinced.*

chunks of bread and cold meat, which she'd brought with her. Val filled her water flask from a small brick-lined well positioned in a corner of the chamber, and then handed it round. Meanwhile, Isi went around the room lighting the wall torches with her own. The fully illuminated vault astonished Lucius all over again. He saw now the rich detail of the mosaics on the walls and how they told, in stages, the story of the city's founding legend – baby twins adrift on the Tiber in a basket, then being suckled by the she-wolf; the killing of the usurper King Amulius; Romulus's sighting of twelve vultures, which convinced him to found the city on the Palatine; the twins' quarrel and the slaying of Remus; Romulus's marking of the city boundaries with a plough; and, finally, old King Romulus with long beard and iron crown, ascending to the heavens during a storm.

So mesmerised was Lucius by these images and the tale they told, he almost failed to heed Isi as she began to explain the situation to them.

'We'll be safe here,' she was saying, 'at least for a while. Everyone will assume we're heading out of the city. This is the last place they'll look. As the priest was saying, it's virtually unknown – despite being, in Quin's words, right under the noses of our enemies.'

'Can someone please explain to me and Lu what happened back at the ludus?' demanded Quin. 'Sergius, Hilario, why didn't you open our cell door? Isi, how come your diversion plan didn't work? And

Val…' He screwed up his face in an effort to conjure up a sufficiently all-encompassing question, but ultimately all he could manage was: '…how?'

Val laughed at his confusion. 'Gajadhar, the slave you met?' she said through a mouthful of half-chewed bread. 'He helped me escape, and I came straight to the ludus because I knew you were there. Isi and I have been corresponding for weeks, swapping messages via Simio.' Lucius smiled at the mention of Val's trusty sidekick Simio, the chimpanzee who had escaped from the vivarium.

Sergius piped up at this point. 'We couldn't get to you two,' he said to Quin and Lucius. 'We're really sorry. Your corridor was too full of guards. When we explained the situation to your sister, she…'

'I told Gajadhar to go and fetch Magnentia,' finished Val. 'You can probably figure out the rest.'

'Not quite,' said Quin, turning back to Hilario. 'What about the other gladiators? How come they were ambushed by Praetorians the moment they got out of the ludus?'

'That was sheer bad luck,' growled Hilario. 'We ran into a cohort of them. Or perhaps they were waiting for us there because of what happened in the ludus this morning. A few of us managed to get away, but the majority fell into the trap. Last I saw, it wasn't looking good. Chances are, they'll all be back in the ludus by now.' He sighed. 'And the punishments are going to be severe. A lot of veteres* will wake up tomorrow morning as damnati.'

'Your diversionary tactic didn't work, then?' Quin said to Isi. He looked flushed with anger, which Lucius thought was somewhat unmerited, considering all that Isi had done for them tonight.

'I did what I could,' she said quietly. 'Clearly, it wasn't enough.'

Quin wasn't finished with his interrogations. Next in his sights was Hector, who'd been silent so far. 'And what are you doing here, Mr Primus Palus?' he challenged him. 'I thought you'd be busy breaking rebel heads back at the ludus, like you were this morning.'

'Had a change of heart,' muttered Hector glumly. 'I was *persuaded*, shall we say, by Hilario here, that my interests might be better served if I joined him in his little adventure tonight.' He turned on Hilario, his voice growing louder and increasingly eaten through with bitterness. 'This ludus is finished, you told me! Crassus is finished! I'd be best off pinning my eagle to a different standard if I want to maintain my status as "most successful Secutor currently on the circuit". That's what you said, wasn't it, Hilario? Well, I have to say, the ludus didn't look very finished tonight, did it – as we fled in fear of our lives from those Praetorians? Crassus didn't look very finished tonight as he and his guardsmen tore into the rebel lines. The only person

* *veteres: veterans, experienced fighters.*

who's finished around here is me! I can tell you now, I won't be primus palus tomorrow. Fact! It won't be *me* taking the victory palm at the Roman Games. Fact! My life is over thanks to you, Hilario. A long and glittering career has just nose-dived into the dust. I hope you can sleep for all the guilt you should be feeling.'

'If it means no longer having to listen to you brag, I shall sleep like a baby, thanks,' chuckled Hilario.

Hearing this, Hector let out a snarl and grabbed Hilario by the scruff of his tunic. 'You swine. I'll kill you for that!' With his other hand, he drew six inches of gleaming blade from his belt. But before he could drive it into Hilario's belly, Quin leapt up and kicked the knife from his hand. The knife went spinning high in the air and was caught by Isi.

'Enough!' she cried, sheathing the knife in her belt. 'The whole world out there wants us dead. All we've got is each other. What chance do we have if we start fighting? Hector, if you want to stay with us, then you'll have to lose the resentful attitude. I want to see you embrace Hilario.'

Hector spat on the floor. 'Never!'

'Then you can leave,' said Isi.

He stared at her, shocked, and Isi stared back.

Quin broke the silence. 'No one's leaving,' he said.

Isi turned on Quin, eyebrows raised at this defiance of her decision.

'I'll kill him if you like,' said Quin with a nod

towards Hector. 'But I'm not letting him out of here. He'll give away our location.'

'Now wait a minute…' cried Hector, alarmed.

'Then perhaps we should put it to a vote,' said Isi, ignoring him. 'All those in favour of Hector leaving, raise your hands.'

Isi raised hers, followed by Hilario. But no one else did. Lucius felt torn. He would gladly have seen the back of Hector, but Quin had a point: he was more dangerous to them out there than in here.

'OK,' said Isi. 'Now all those who think he should stay…'

Lucius put up his hand, and so did Quin, Sergius, Val and Faustina.

'Fine!' said Isi, managing to conceal the disappointment she must have felt. 'It appears you are to remain with us, Hector. But you'd better behave yourself, or I may be forced to ask Quin to carry out his threat.'

Hector scowled. 'In that case, give me back my knife so I can defend myself.'

Isi shook her head. 'I'll keep the knife until you've proved yourself an honourable and trustworthy member of the group.'

Sullenly, Hector lowered himself back to the floor.

Lucius was astonished at how naturally Isi had adopted the role of leader of their group. It was a quality he'd not really noticed in her before, yet she seemed to wear it well. And Hector, the big, brawny tyrant of the ludus, had accepted her authority as meekly as a lamb. It reminded him of her pacifying effect on Kato, the ferocious tiger, back when they were working at the vivarium.

Isi had saved them tonight. Val and Magnentia had helped, too, of course. But Isi had been the main organiser, from ensuring that the ludus entrance was unguarded to finding them a place of sanctuary. No one asked about what they would do tomorrow or the next day, but somehow Lucius reckoned that those issues would take care of themselves. For the time being at least, they were safe.

With the issue of their immediate survival resolved, the group prepared to settle down for the night, using their cloaks as mattresses on the hard stone floor. Hilario complained of the cold, now he'd divested himself of his cloak. Lucius, who had made his 'bed' next to him, offered his own, and the cheerful, broken-nosed Provocator gladly accepted it. Within minutes, he was quietly snoring.

Lucius observed Isi seated opposite him, conversing quietly with Faustina, her expression anxious yet determined to appear composed, and he felt an overwhelming need to express his appreciation to her. He would have got up and gone over to her, except that his chest felt too tender for any further exertion.

'Isi!' he called.

She turned and looked at him.

'Thank you,' he smiled at her.

Noticing the pain that must have been clouding his eyes, she immediately rose and went to him.

'How are you feeling?' she asked. 'How's the wound?'

He enjoyed her closeness, her woody, amber scent.

'I daren't look,' he said. 'I think some of the stitching may have broken... But I just wanted to tell you how grateful I am, and Quin is, for what you did for us tonight. I don't think that came across in the way he was questioning you before, but he's grateful, I know he is. And so am I.'

'Don't worry about it,' she said. 'It was the least I could do. You two have been through much worse times than me. Beaten within an inch of your lives, threatened with a horrible death, and forced to fight without armour. I was there at the amphitheatre this afternoon when you fought the Dacian. You were amazingly brave and quick. I was in awe of you.'

Lucius's heart beat faster at these words. Warmth flooded his cheeks. Before he could think of how to reply, Faustina came over to them with her bag. She kneeled down by Lucius. 'Let me take a look at your chest,' she said. 'I used to assist Eumenes back at the ludus, and picked up a little medical know-how.'

'I told her to bring some bandages and creams,' said Isi, '– reckoned you'd probably need it.'

'Thank you,' said Lucius, and he opened up the top of his tunic so Faustina could examine him. Carefully, she unwound the bloodstained bandages. The exposed wound was a swollen angry pink at its edges, with blood and some pus seeping out where the stitching had broken at one end – but it didn't look half as bad as Lucius had feared. Faustina used a cotton swab soaked in turpentine to dab away the blood and pus. Lucius clenched his fists against the streaks of sharp pain as the pungent oil entered the tender lip of the wound.

Val came over and knelt close to him. 'Be brave, Lu,' she whispered, kissing his cheek.

Lucius attempted a reassuring smile. 'I'll be fine,' he said. 'Go and talk to Quin. We've got so much catching up to do. I'll be over later.'

The truth was, he didn't want his sister to see him in pain.

Val nodded and left, and Lucius turned to see Faustina rummaging around in her bag. He gasped as he saw her take out a box of bone needles of varying sizes, and a ball of wool.

'Eumenes gave me opium before he stitched me up,' he said to her.

Faustina smiled regretfully at him. 'I don't have opium. But I must close it up at the end. Just three or four stitches. I'll work as quick as I can.'

Isi clasped his hand tightly. 'I'll be here for you,' she said. 'Squeeze my hand as hard as you like, I don't mind.'

The pain of the next few minutes was searing. He screwed up his eyes and his cheeks grew moist with tears. He was barely aware of how hard he was squeezing Isi's hand – he hoped he wasn't hurting her – but she never made a sound.

When it was over, and the wound had been dressed in fresh bandages, Lucius lay back on a blanket that Faustina had kindly lent him, and Val and Quin came over to see how he was doing.

Lucius could immediately see that something was upsetting Quin.

'What's wrong?' he asked.

Quin glanced over his shoulder to make sure no one else was listening. 'Val's just told me that Mother is shortly to marry Glabrio,' he muttered. 'The wedding is due to take place in two weeks.'

Lucius felt hollow inside. He let out a long breath. 'I'm afraid she's lost to us now,' he said. 'She's no longer our mother.'

'I totally agree,' said Quin.

'She'll always be our mother,' declared Val defiantly. 'She's just misguided, that's all. I've tried talking to her, giving her hints about what sort of man he is, but she never hears me out. She just interrupts or storms out of the room. But if all three of us were to try and convince her...'

Lucius exchanged a glance with Quin. 'Shall we tell her?' he murmured.

Val was looking from one brother to the other with growing alarm. 'Tell me what? What do you know?'

Quin nodded.

'Oh, Val,' sighed Lucius. 'I'm so sorry to have to tell you this, but…'

'But what?'

'Mother isn't quite the innocent we all assumed her to be… The man we met in Britannia, the one who gave us the autopsy report we were going to use to bring down Glabrio – Parmenion, his name was. He told us a few things about… about Mother.'

Lucius told her what Parmenion had discovered during one of his visits to Glabrio's house: that their mother, Caecilia, had been a regular visitor to Glabrio's house, and possibly his bedroom, before Aquila's death, and that she had known in advance about the plot to kill the emperor Titus.

Val cried out in shock when she heard this. 'No! I can't believe it!'

'That was my reaction at first,' said Quin. 'But then I thought about it a bit more – about how she opposed Father's visit to the emperor's villa, and his planned speech to the Senate revealing the emperor's murder, and how she flew off to Glabrio's house that night – obviously with the intention of warning him of what Father was about to do.'

By now Val was in tears. 'Are you saying she was behind Father's murder too?' she sobbed.

'No, of course not!' said Quin sharply. 'She couldn't have had any idea how Glabrio would react when she told him.'

He frowned – and Lucius swallowed uncomfortably.

The horrid suspicion had hit all three of them: was it possible that their mother had connived at her own husband's death? They knew that for many years there had been little love between Aquila and Caecilia, and she had failed to show any loyalty to him when false accusations had driven him into exile. Even so, it was another kind of evil entirely to actually conspire to kill him. And it made her their enemy, just as surely as Glabrio was. None of them was prepared to go that far.

The light drained from the room and the shadows expanded as Isi and Sergius doused the wall torches one by one, leaving just one flickering faintly on the far side of the grotto.

'All this makes me even more certain that my place is now with you,' sniffed Val. 'I'd sooner die than live under that man's roof again.'

Lucius could barely see his sister's face now. The murmur of voices around the room had ceased as the others drifted into sleep. The only sound was the faint, echoing splashes coming from the well. He imagined the tiny drops gathering on the wet base of the bucket and then plunging down that black shaft of ancient bricks and shattering on the still, inky surface far below. It reminded Lucius more forcefully than ever of the bleak future that awaited them. He couldn't bear the thought of Val joining their almost certainly doomed struggle.

'There may be no way back now for me and Quin,'

he said softly to her, 'but you've still got everything to live for, Val. You *have* to go back. I want you to grow up and marry and lead a happy life. At least one of us Valerii must survive.'

Val shook her head vigorously. 'No way am I going back there,' she vowed. 'I can't bear the thought of living in the house of a murderer. And I know he's a murderer for sure now because I heard it from Aleta, one of the kitchen slaves.'

'You heard what, exactly?' asked Lucius, intrigued.

'Aleta told me she was there at the emperor's villa on the day he was murdered. She'd gone there as part of Glabrio's personal retinue. She actually saw Glabrio order the cook to poison the sea-hare that killed Titus.'

'Would she be prepared to stand up and say that in court?' asked Lucius.

'I asked her and she looked petrified by the idea,' said Val. 'She's a frail old Greek lady, and she's worked for Glabrio long enough to know how ruthless he is.'

'I doubt it would do us any good anyway,' said Quin. 'Who'd ever believe the word of a slave against a man of Glabrio's rank?' He yawned. 'I'm exhausted, aren't you two? We should get some kip.'

They said goodnight and crawled onto their makeshift beds. Lucius thought about what Val had said about Aleta. Was this a new ray of hope, or another false dawn? He'd grown tired of a struggle in which every path they followed seemed to lead to new defeats and yet more painful punishments. The only positive was that they were still alive, and they were together. Tomorrow they'd decide on a new strategy. He shivered. With the torches doused, their subterranean haven had definitely grown chillier, and now he regretted giving Hilario his cloak. He tried to draw part of his blanket-mattress around his body, but the movement sent another bolt of pain through his chest. Soon, he gave up and simply waited for sleep to come. Within a few minutes, it did.

Lucius awoke to the sound of screams – howling, hysterical screams. Wondering if he was dreaming, he blinked a few times and opened his eyes. The screams continued as loudly as ever, so he levered himself quickly into an upright position – too quickly for his wound, which complained sharply at the movement.

'Dead!' moaned the voice. 'He's dead!' It sounded like Faustina.

Other voices now broke in.

'Who's dead?' demanded Isi.

'What's going on?' groaned Sergius.

Lucius turned to see Faustina standing over Hilario's bed with a lit torch. 'Poor man!' she whimpered.

Lucius stared. In the flickering light he could see Hilario's eyes wide open, gazing at nothing. His neck was covered in bruises.

'He was murdered,' said Lucius.

CHAPTER IX

7–8 SEPTEMBER

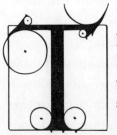he room erupted with startled cries. People leapt to their feet, more torches were lit and everyone began speaking at once.

'Hush!' screamed Isi in a voice loud and shrill enough to be heard above everyone else's.

When the room was quiet and still again, she walked over to Hilario's body and crouched down beside it. Feeling his cheek, she murmured: 'He's stone cold. Must have been dead for hours…' She noted the neck bruises. 'Looks like Lucius was right. He was strangled.'

This provoked more shocked gasps from Val and Sergius. Faustina began quietly sobbing.

'There are two possibilities,' said Isi, scanning everyone's face in turn. 'Either an outsider came in here and did this while we were asleep, or... or one of *us* killed him.'

'I don't know why you're trying to turn this into some big mystery,' said Quin. 'It's obvious who did it.'

He was looking intensely at Hector, who was sitting calmly against the wall, picking at something in his teeth. If the Secutor sensed that he'd suddenly become the centre of everyone's attention, he was doing a good job of ignoring it.

'We all saw him threaten Hilario last night,' continued Quin. 'Isi may have confiscated his knife, but that didn't stop him using his hands.'

'What do you say, Hector?' asked Isi.

Hector looked up at her, aghast. 'You're not taking that lunatic's ravings seriously, are you?' he shouted. 'Of course I didn't kill Hilario.' He clambered to his feet, reminding everyone of his intimidating height and bulk. 'Has it occurred to you why he might be flinging these accusations, hm? It's to distract attention from himself: the real murderer.'

Quin made a scoffing sound. 'That's ridiculous,' he said. 'Why should I kill Hilario? I liked the fellow.'

'Yeah,' said Hector, pointing an accusing finger at Quin's face. 'And you *hate* me. I know you've had it in for me ever since you came to the ludus – always looking for ways to put me down in front of others. You knew that if you killed Hilario, everyone would think I'd done it. This is just your latest attempt to ruin me. Well, it's not going to work.'

Quin's eyes bulged in disbelief when he heard this. 'Kill an innocent man to spite someone else?' he chuckled drily. 'Now I've heard it all!'

Isi shook her head. 'I *know* Quin, and he would never do that,' she said. 'Don't forget, he gave up being a gladiator because he hated all the killing.'

'Or because he lost his nerve,' sneered Hector. 'But it's one thing facing an armed man in an arena, and another strangling an unarmed one while he's asleep. Even a coward like Quin can manage that.'

This was too much for Quin, who let fly with his fist at Hector's face. There was a crunching sound and Hector let out a roar of pain, clamping his hand over his nose. When he removed it, blood was streaming from both nostrils and coating his lips. 'So much for your vow of non-violence,' he leered through blood-stained teeth. 'Or did I get too close to the truth for your liking?'

'Stop it!' yelled Sergius, clutching his head in exasperation. 'Stop it, both of you! This is not a time for fighting and arguing. We are a familia – for better or worse, we must stay friends. A man has died tonight – a man I loved like a brother. We must show him respect. We must bury him.'

He stepped closer to Hilario and knelt close to him. Tenderly, he touched his face, closing his too-wide eyes, drawing the curtains on a life. Lucius could see that Sergius was trying very hard not to cry. 'This whole thing began with Hilario,' he said in a tight, wavering voice. 'This rebellion. He'd had enough... of the disrespect, the bad food. All he wanted... all he wanted was to be treated fairly. To be shown some consideration. I don't know why anyone would want to... to snuff out the life of someone... so full of life.'

Sergius broke down, and had to be led gently away by Faustina.

Lucius then approached the body. He was about to retrieve his cloak when his hand froze. 'My cloak,' he said through shuddering lips. 'He was wearing my cloak.' He turned to face the others. 'Whoever killed him may have been trying to kill me.'

'Let's not jump to any conclusions,' said Isi, trying to stay calm. 'We're all a bit on edge at the moment. Let's just...'

There was a sound of creaking hinges. She turned, and flinched slightly at the sight of the priest standing there at the top of the steps. He stared balefully at them. 'Last night,' he said, 'I asked you all to treat this shrine with respect. Now I understand that someone has seen fit to commit murder in here. This... is.... desecration!'

'Can you be sure no one came in here while we slept?' Isi asked him.

'I guard the door,' said the priest sternly. 'No one came in here last night.'

'Do you never sleep?' asked Val in a tremulous voice.

He glared at her with his implacable yellow eyes. '*No one* came in here last night!'

'We'll... we'll make a contribution, a financial contribution,' said Isi desperately, clearly sensing, as Lucius did, that the priest was on the point of throwing them out. 'But please let us stay here just a little longer. It's not safe for us to leave yet.'

The priest considered this a moment before giving a brief nod: 'All right. But this is your last chance.' He turned and disappeared through the little wooden door.

Silence reigned in the chamber, until Val piped up that she was hungry. Faustina offered to go and buy breakfast. The others handed her some coins and off she went.

Lucius kept Sergius company while they waited for Faustina to return. The lad seemed to have taken Hilario's death very badly.

'Hilario was the first person at the ludus to show me real kindness,' Sergius told him. 'Maybe the first person ever, apart from my mother. I shall miss him.'

Lucius nodded. 'Me, too.'

'He was the only one I told, apart from you, about that secret room I lived in before I joined the ludus. Remember that room I told you about? I knew he wouldn't tell anyone. I could trust him, like I can trust you.' Sergius chuckled sadly. 'All he said to me was: "You mean you actually *stole* food from the ludus kitchens? You risked your life to steal the muck they give us?" He couldn't believe I'd do that. But I didn't find it so bad. I quite enjoyed my days in the secret room.' Sergius looked around him. 'Maybe that's why I don't mind it here. It reminds me of that place.'

'What, you mean it was full of fancy mosaics?'

'No,' said Sergius. 'I mean it was underground.'

When Faustina reappeared an hour or so later laden with bread rolls, cheese and grapes, she reported that the streets were teeming with Praetorian patrols on foot and on horseback. 'I saw house-to-house searches,' said Faustina, 'and they were stopping people in the street and interrogating them. Glabrio must have given orders to leave no stone unturned in this city until you are found.'

Hector looked up from his cheese roll. 'Glabrio? Why should *he* be bothered by a few runaway gladiators?'

Faustina glanced in sudden panic at Isi, worried she might have said too much.

Hector's eyes grew sharp with suspicion. 'Are you lot in trouble over something else, then?'

'Who gave you leave to talk to us?' Quin yelled at him. 'Keep your trap shut unless you want another taste of my fist.'

'Enough, Quin!' snapped Isi.

Hector smirked at Quin. 'So you *have* got something to hide, then?'

'Wouldn't you love to know?' said Quin. 'I've seen how tight you are with the ludus authorities – how you've got Crassus eating out of your hand. I wouldn't be surprised if you weren't Glabrio's spy.'

Hector bristled at the accusation. 'I don't work for Glabrio, and I'm no one's spy. Fact! I just want to know what's going on. I know you two are damnati, but I haven't a clue what crime you committed. If you've made an enemy of Glabrio, then I want to know about it – because that's one guy I'd rather not get on the wrong side of.'

'He owns the ludus,' said Isi. 'You lot are his property, and he wants you back. That's all there is to it.'

A tense and uncomfortable peace reigned in the Lupercal for the rest of that day. Lucius, Quin and Val spent the time catching up on news, murmuring in low voices to each other out of earshot of Hector and Sergius. Val was amazed by Lucius's tales of Carthage and Ephesus, and listened wide-eyed as he and Quin related their adventures in Britannia. She told them about her dull and restricted existence in Glabrio's town house, where she couldn't go anywhere without being observed by the master's slave-spies. Her only solace was the animals: Argos, Lucius's dog, as well as Simio, Magnentia and the tiger, Kato, who she said were all thriving in their enclosures within the extensive grounds of the property.

Isi and Faustina joined them after a time, causing an awkward split in the group, with Sergius and Hector on one side of the room and everyone else on the other. Val enjoyed being in her brothers' company so much that soon she began to forget about their circumstances. At one point, she burst out laughing at something Quin said. Her laughter died quickly, though, leaving just its echo ringing around the mosaic-covered walls.

'I'm glad you find this situation so amusing,' shouted Sergius angrily, gesturing towards Hilario's corpse. 'Perhaps you'd like to share the joke with him.'

'I'm sorry,' murmured Val.

There was no further laughter that day.

There was no means of measuring the passage of time in the Lupercal, except for the swelling hunger in their bellies and the need every few hours to add tinder to the torches – storage jars filled with dry tree bark and pitch had been provided for the purpose. Faustina was their link with the outside world, fetching them food and news on Praetorian activity. In the evening, she returned with a meal of hard-boiled eggs, dried fish, apples and wine. She even managed to obtain a jar of garum, the fish sauce that Val liked so much.

'It's dark outside,' Faustina reported. 'It will be safe now to bury Hilario.'

After they had finished their meal, Sergius and

Quin hoisted up Hilario between them, and the seven fugitives mounted the steps and ventured back into the tunnel. The priest met them there, handing spades to Faustina, Isi and Hector. Then they progressed solemnly along the tunnel, managing, with some careful manoeuvring, to get Hilario's body through the crack in the wall. Isi selected a suitable site for the burial in the verdant wilderness at the base of the palace ramparts. It was reasonably flat, and also concealed from the public gaze by some giant ferns. They got to work on the grave, taking it in turns to dig into the moist soil, dense with plant roots. Lucius, excused from digging duty because of his wound, kept watch, hissing warnings if he spotted any pedestrians coming or going along the Vicus Consinius below.

Eventually, a rectangular hole long and wide enough to accommodate Hilario's bulk was excavated. Sergius placed a silver coin in Hilario's mouth so that he could pay Charon the ferryman, who would take his soul across the River Styx to the underworld, and they placed his body in the four-foot-deep hole. Sergius gave a short laudatio funebris, or funeral oration. He wept as he recounted the Provocator's triumphs in the arena, and chuckled through his tears as he recalled his dry sense of humour. He poured a libation of wine into the soil next to the grave. Then the others got to work with their spades, hastily refilling the hole.

Back in the vault, everyone began settling down for a second night underground. The tension was felt by all, though no one spoke of it. Whoever had killed Hilario might kill again tonight. If so, who would the victim be this time?

'We should mount a watch,' said Isi. 'Two at a time, so the killer – if one of us is the killer – is never on guard by himself. I'll go first. Who would like to join me?'

Quin immediately volunteered.

'Good,' said Isi. 'And when the night torch starts to gutter, we'll wake up the next pair.'

'Hector and I can do that one,' said Sergius.

Hector hesitated, then nodded his assent.

'Watch your co-watcher closely,' Quin warned Sergius in a low voice.

'I can do the final watch with Faustina,' said Lucius.

'What about me?' piped up Val.

'You can enjoy a nice sleep, my dear,' smiled Faustina.

Lucius snuggled down on his blanket, grateful for the warmth of the cloak that covered his body. In the night torch's flickering light he could make out the forms of Isi and Quin, sitting with their backs against the wall. Quin's eyes, he noticed, never strayed from Hector. Lucius knew it would be a struggle to sleep tonight. The idea of there being a killer in their midst put his nerves on edge. He considered the potential suspects. It had to be Hector, surely. Who else? Sergius? But Sergius had loved Hilario. Yet what if he'd mistaken Hilario for *him* – Lucius – because of the cloak? Lucius couldn't imagine why Sergius would want to kill him, though. He'd been so friendly, seemed almost to idolise him. So who else? Faustina? Definitely not! The priest? Now there was a possibility. He was a strange one, for sure, with those yellow, wolf-like eyes. Perhaps spending his life underground had affected his mind. Perhaps he was planning to pick them all off one by one. The thought made Lucius shudder and he pulled the cloak more tightly around his neck. He glanced fearfully towards the little wooden door at the top of the steps. If that door opened now, he would simply die of fright. Yet he dared not take his eyes off it. He wished he had a weapon with him – something to protect himself with, just in case.

He got to his knees and began feeling with his fingers up the wall. Climbing to his feet, he discerned the outline of one of the wall brackets that held the torches. He grasped the doused torch and pulled it from its iron cradle. It was a flimsy thing – a bunch of thin wooden staves bound with twine – but better than nothing. Feeling a little more secure, he returned to a horizontal position, placing the torch between himself and the wall behind. Then he continued his vigil over the little wooden door. Many minutes went by. The door didn't open. Nothing moved in the room. There was no sound except for gentle breathing and the faint drips from the well. He yawned. It was becoming a struggle to keep his eyes open. Perhaps he could just shut them for a few minutes... Just to give them a rest... then he would...

He was in the arena. The Dacian was standing before him, carving up the air between them with his curved sword. The blade slashed close, so close Lucius could feel the air parting around it, and it sounded like the whisper of death. He could almost feel the agony of its bite, and see his skin opening like a curtain, revealing parts of him that should never see the light of day. Lucius tried to jerk away from the dancing blade – yet he felt restricted, as if bound in tight cloth. He couldn't move as he wished to. The Dacian advanced and his blade became a spinning, whirling, deadly blur. Lucius kicked outwards in terror and the sword flew up into the sky, revolving as it went until it was caught by Isi, who was seated high up in the stands, watching him. From somewhere nearby came the echoing splash of water. He turned wildly, but could only see a blur of hot, dry sand and faces. The Dacian, furious now, came at Lucius with his huge hands. He clamped them around Lucius's neck and began to squeeze. Lucius felt the pressure build. He coughed and choked. He tried to prise the hands from his neck, but they were too strong. He could hear the Dacian grunting with effort. He couldn't breathe. He...

Lucius's eyes flew open. The squeezing on his neck – it was real! Some powerful, terrifying presence was crouched over him in the dark, throttling him. The pain was terrible. He tried to scream, but nothing came out. The fingers were like iron clamps around his throat – unmovable! He tried to suck in air, but could get nothing. No air. It was like that time when he had nearly drowned in the Pontine Marshes. He

flailed about, trying to shake off his attacker. He had
to get air! But he had no strength. He could hear his
own feeble grunting in his ears – like a piglet being
strangled at birth. His lungs became hard and dry as
sunbaked stones. No air! He was reaching the end.
White spots appeared before his eyes. He twisted
with the last of his energy. His hand closed around
something – something wooden – the torch! He jerked
it upwards. There was a distant crack above him – the
sound of wood against skull – then a groan.

The tightness around his throat eased. Air screamed
into his parched, dry lungs. Lucius whipped the torch
in another blind arc, but this time the other end was
caught in one of the hands that had so nearly killed him.
He tried to tug it free, but couldn't. So he let go and
rose clumsily to his feet, wheezing like a long-distance
Olympic runner. There was a clatter as the torch fell to
the ground. He groped around, trying to connect with
his attacker. The darkness in the room was absolute
– the killer must have extinguished the night torch.
Footsteps raced away from him across the stone floor.
Then a light flared, and he saw Faustina's anxious face
squinting at him from the far side of the room.

'Lucius? Is that you? What happened? Are you
all right?'

More torches were lit. Lucius fell to the ground.
His vision was blurred, his throat on fire, and
breathing was like sucking air through a narrow reed
half-blocked with mud. He sensed people around

him, staring at him, their voices filled with panic and concern, but he found it hard to make out what they were saying. He could hear Val crying, and wanted more than anything for her to be away from this hell they had found themselves in.

Gradually, breathing became easier. His vision started to clear, and the sounds became more comprehensible. Isi loomed close and he heard her ask him: 'Who did it, Lu? Did you catch sight of him?'

Lucius shook his head. Speech was beyond him.

'Sergius, what happened?' shouted Quin. 'You and Hector were supposed to be on guard.'

'I'm so sorry,' said a dazed-looking Sergius. 'I must have fallen asleep. Where… Where is Hector?'

They looked around them.

Hector was gone.

CHAPTER X

8–15 SEPTEMBER

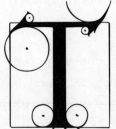hey searched for Hector in every niche
and recess of the chamber, but he was
nowhere to be found. Nor could they
find any trace of him in the passage
outside. They found the priest lying
in his bed in a little room carved out of the rock in
the tunnel wall, close to the entrance to the Lupercal.
Bleary-eyed, the priest swore he hadn't seen or heard
anything, but had to admit that he'd been asleep.

When Isi told him what had just happened, he sat
up sharply. 'You must go!' he said. 'Now!'

'We will,' Isi assured him. 'We're not safe here
anyway – not now. He may well have given away our
location.'

Lucius's neck ached, and bruising was already

187

starting to appear around his throat. He wished now that he'd taken off after Hector before he'd got away. If he'd acted faster, he could have tackled him and brought him down. Then he remembered his chest wound and realised that he was in no state to act the hero. Impotent anger burned in his veins at the Secutor's cowardly attack. He wanted revenge – but he also wanted to interrogate him, to find out the reason for the attack. Hector had barely been aware of Lucius's existence until their escape two nights ago. Or was this all about getting back at Quin? Too chicken-hearted to attack Quin directly, had he decided to pick off his nearest and dearest instead? Lucius shuddered at the thought that Hector might have chosen to attack Val instead of him.

'You should have let me have it out with him yesterday,' Quin growled at Isi as they returned to the chamber to pack up their things. 'You were too fair-minded – and now not only did he nearly throttle Lucius to death, he's escaped and we're forced to abandon a perfectly good hiding place.'

'And what would you have done to him if I'd let you?' Isi challenged him. 'Murdered him in cold blood? There was no hard evidence that he killed Hilario.'

'Evidence!' scowled Quin. 'You're sounding more and more like that ridiculous young lawyer, Gaius. What more evidence do you need? He's escaped, hasn't he?'

'I'm talking about yesterday,' said Isi through

gritted teeth. 'I didn't know he was going to escape then, did I? So tell me, what would you have done, Quin? You weren't prepared to let him go. I'll grant you were probably right about that. So what then? Would you have executed him? And if so, how does that make you any better than Glabrio?'

The two of them faced each other across the floor of the chamber. Isi's face was tilted upwards, her cheeks aflame, her jaw tight with indignation. Quin looked down, and for a moment Lucius thought he might concede the argument. But then he met her gaze and said: 'I'd have challenged him to a fight to the death.'

Isi nodded and smiled. 'Your answer to everything, Quin: if in doubt, use your fists. And what if he'd killed you? That would have suited you, wouldn't it? Your hero status would have been preserved. But you'd have left the rest of us in the company of a man you believe is a killer – your brother, your sister, the people you care about, all suddenly a lot more vulnerable. What kind of a solution is that?'

Quin glowered at her and turned away. 'Come on,' he said, shouldering the bag of their remaining provisions. 'We should get out of here before sunrise.'

Faustina offered them temporary shelter at her apartment, at least until they could find themselves a safer hiding place – so that was where they now headed. They walked north through the dark, slumbering city towards her insula* on the Quirinal Hill, taking backstreets and avoiding the main thoroughfares and squares.

Lucius's breathing improved once they were out in the open air, but his chest wound was aching again and he was forced to ask the others to slow down. By the time they reached Faustina's apartment, an hour and a half later, the first colours of dawn – pale yellow, rose and violet – were glowing through the mist above the Viminal Hill to the east. It felt crowded with six of them in Faustina's modest living room. She fussed around them, distributing stools and cushions for people to sit on, opening shutters and clearing space on the table for their breakfast.

After they had eaten, they began discussing their next move. Sergius was all in favour of abandoning Rome and trying their luck in another city. 'We could sign up as gladiators in a new ludus,' he said. 'Under false names, of course. It'll be *really* exciting, being someone else!'

The others looked at him, not knowing quite what to say. Could he be trusted with the truth? He seemed innocent enough – almost too innocent. They couldn't work out what his reaction would be. Would he run straight to the authorities? Eventually, Lucius said: 'Sergius, we're not interested in being gladiators any more.'

His face fell. 'Really? But that's all I want to do.

* *insula: multistorey apartment block.*

And...' He looked down at his crossed ankles and dirty sandals. 'Now that Hilario's dead, and... and Hector has proved himself a villain... you guys are all I have left.'

Lucius glanced at Isi, who shook her head firmly. He looked at Quin, who was smiling kindly at Sergius. 'You want to join our gang, do you, Sergius?' Quin asked.

Sergius looked up at him eagerly. 'I kind of thought I already had, but... yes. Yes, I do.'

'You're not part of it yet because you don't know everything,' said Quin. 'You don't know our big secret.'

'Quin!' said Isi, giving him a hard stare.

Quin ignored her. 'We want to bring down Glabrio,' he said simply.

'The consul?' gasped Sergius. 'So Hector was right. There *is* some kind of bad blood between you guys and him.'

'He killed our father,' said Val.

'He also murdered Emperor Titus,' added Lucius.

'No!' said Sergius.

'He's an enemy of Rome,' said Quin. 'He must be destroyed. Do you want to help?'

'I...' Sergius looked stunned. 'Yes I do. But... does Glabrio know you're after him?'

'Yes,' said Quin. 'He's been trying to kill us. When he couldn't do that, he bribed witnesses to give false testimony against us at a trial, which was how we ended up as damnati at the ludus.'

Sergius nodded slowly. 'So if I join with you guys, I'll be in even more trouble than I was yesterday.'

'You're already in deep trouble,' said Quin bluntly. 'If you get captured now, Glabrio will assume you're one of us.'

'I'm sorry, Sergius,' said Lucius. 'This must be a lot more than you bargained for when you joined the great escape.'

'It's OK,' said Sergius, swallowing drily. 'I know what it's like to hate. Watching your drunk father smash his fist into your mother's face, hearing the snap of her nose breaking – it teaches you that. So I understand how you must hate Glabrio. Ever since I ran away from home, I've been looking for an alternative – a place where I feel I can belong. I joined the ludus, but… maybe that wasn't right either. It just replaced one kind of mindless brutality with another. I'm a good fighter, though – my experiences have taught me that much. Maybe what I need is a cause worth fighting for… I like you people. I liked you from the moment I met you. So count me in.'

'Welcome,' beamed Quin.

Isi bit her lip, but said nothing.

They spent eight days at Faustina's. It was a testing time. The apartment felt cramped with the six of them, and Quin especially found the enforced inactivity hard to bear. As for Faustina, although she never complained and was a tirelessly welcoming hostess, Lucius could tell from the increasing tightness and weariness of her smile that she missed having the place to herself. Nevertheless, it was a necessary precaution as the streets continued to swarm and bristle with hyper-vigilant Praetorian search patrols. As Lucius kept telling himself, it was better to be bored and free than bored and waiting to die in some stinking cell.

They found ways of passing the time. Quin and Valeria would play epic tournaments of latrunculi, their favourite board game. Lucius would lie on cushions reading cheaply made papyrus works of philosophy and history bought for him by Faustina at a nearby bookshop. She also bought hemp for Sergius, who set about braiding the strands together to make a length of rope – a hobby he'd taught himself as a boy. When he wasn't making rope, Sergius joined Val and Faustina in Isi's regular exercise classes. Isi would move aside the table in the living room to create some space, and then would train them in the arts of balance, stretching and flexibility – skills she herself had learned from her former boss and mentor, Hierax. Quin preferred to exercise alone, unwilling perhaps to receive instruction, or anything else, from Isi. Relations between the two of them remained frosty, with both competing for the unofficial title of leader of the group.

When Sergius had completed a rope of reasonable

length, he began demonstrating to anyone interested the art of the laqueus, or lasso. He made a loop out of one end of the rope and secured the other end around his wrist, then flung the looped end around a target and pulled, tightening the noose. For a while, he, Val and Quin practised enthusiastically on an amphora,* a lamp and a bronze figurine placed on the table. Faustina was forced to put a stop to this activity, however, after Quin broke a jug that had belonged to her late lamented grandmother.

Lucius was the only one who was unable to take part in these physical pursuits. This was mildly frustrating for him, but he was grateful in other ways for this period of involuntary idleness, as it allowed his chest wound to heal. After several days of lying around on comfortable cushions and receiving regular medical attention from Faustina, Lucius was definitely feeling a lot better, and by the fifth day he was even able to join Isi's class for some light stretching exercises.

Inaction also gave Lucius time to think about things, and the thing he seemed to think about most often (apart from Glabrio and how to destroy him, which remained his chief obsession) was Isi. It was maddening being so close to her but unable to actually talk to her in private. Instead, he took to watching her exercise and trying to imagine what was going on in her head. That golden day they'd spent on Lake Albano,

* *amphora: a pottery jug with a pointed end, used for storing wine, oil and foodstuffs.*

194

that kiss they'd shared, seemed like a dream to him now. He could hardly believe it had actually happened, or that he was the person it had happened to. Isi had shown him a different side that day – a warm, tender, loving side. Perhaps she'd even surprised herself. He wished he'd been given time to explore that side of her further. But it had been an altogether different Isi who had organised the rescue from the ludus. These days, her face was like a mask, her eyes hard and focused on practical things. She'd become a leader of their little group, alongside Quin, who did not seem yet to have accepted her authority.

Lucius would have liked to talk to Isi about these things, to try to understand her a bit better. Why, for example, did she get upset when Quin recruited Sergius to the group? Was it just her natural caution – or did she have genuine cause to think Sergius might be a threat to them? If so, he'd have liked to know why she thought that. Most of all, though, he just wanted to be close to her again – as they'd been in those long-ago, carefree days, working together at the ludus and the vivarium. By becoming a leader, she'd had to distance herself from him. He missed their conversations, and he longed for a time, maybe in the future – if they had a future – when they might become proper friends again.

After eight days, Faustina was able to report a lessening of the Praetorian presence on the streets. Quin suggested it was time they ventured out again. He gave Faustina the address of Mutio, an old friend of his who was an expert in the art of disguise. He asked her to call on him and invite him to the apartment with his 'box of tricks'. Once Mutio had performed his magic on them, Quin predicted, they would be able to mingle freely with the Roman crowds.

An hour later, Faustina returned with Mutio. He was a small, grinning man with a dark beard and a gold hoop in his ear, hunched almost double under the weight of the bag he was carrying. He and Quin embraced warmly. 'Good see you, old friend,' said Mutio.

After depositing his bag on the floor, he lifted out a heavy-looking wooden box with brass fittings. Lucius saw, when Mutio opened it, that the interior of the box was divided into small compartments, each crowded with corked bottles, rags, brushes and wax crayons. The little man studied Lucius's face with an expert eye.

'Come sit,' he invited Lucius.

Lucius seated himself on a stool.

'Closer,' urged Mutio. 'I have short arms,' he grinned.

Lucius came closer.

Not taking his eyes off Lucius, Mutio reached for a bottle and a thick brush, then set to work. The man's grin disappeared as he became absorbed in his craft.

His face loomed close enough for Lucius to see the deep pores in his cheeks and the yellow ivory of his narrow teeth behind his bulbous red lips. The brush felt like a feather against his skin, as Mutio laid down some sort of foundation colour. The make-up artist worked quickly, and seemingly by instinct. Picking out bottles and tools without even looking, he daubed and smeared, dabbed and swabbed, touched and wiped, always maintaining his frowning dark-eyed focus on Lucius's face. Sharp, acrid, vinegary smells filled the air. Mutio's face leaned in even closer as sharp lines were applied to the edges of Lucius's eyes and mouth. After a little more dabbing and smearing, he gave a grunt of approval and removed the top tray of his make-up box. Beneath was a second layer filled with wigs, false beards, eyepatches, false ears and noses. He picked out a dark brown, almost black wig for Lucius, which he placed carefully on his head before combing and styling it to his satisfaction. Finally, he took out a bronze mirror and handed it to Lucius.

'You like, yes?' he enquired, the grin reappearing.

Lucius was astonished. It was as if he was looking not into a mirror but through a round window at a completely different person. He understood then that Quin had been a very unsubtle and rudimentary exponent of the art of disguise. He had resorted to crude effects such as false scars and enlarged noses to camouflage a person's face, but they always felt like unnatural additions, and Lucius had never been comfortable wearing them. Mutio, by contrast, had taken note of Lucius's face and used that as his starting point, working with his bone structure, but using subtle effects of colour and shading to distort things like eye, nose and mouth shapes. He'd given him a different face, but Lucius didn't feel awkward or uncomfortable wearing it. He knew he could carry off this disguise – he could become the boy now staring back at him from the mirror.

Mutio spent all morning with them, working his magic on Quin, Isi, Val and Sergius in turn. When he was finished, Faustina clapped her hands and laughed in astonishment. 'If I didn't know better,' she said, 'I would think I suddenly had a houseful of strangers.'

Val admired her wavy red locks and rosy cheeks in the mirror. 'Are we ready to go out now?' she pleaded. 'I really want to go out into town and show off my new look.'

'Of course,' said Quin. 'We're now as safe as we'll ever be.' His golden-blond curls were hidden beneath a brown mop of hair, and his bronzed outdoor complexion, picked up during his months of living on the streets as an augur,* was now several shades lighter, lending him the pallor of that subterranean priest of the Lupercal.

'So what do we do now?' asked Isi after she'd paid

---

* augur: a priest who claimed to be able to interpret the will of the gods by observing natural phenomena such as the flight of birds. Quin had once disguised himself as an augur, with Mutio's help.

Mutio and he'd bid them all farewell. She frowned at
them expectantly. Lucius almost laughed to see her.
Isi was wearing a wig of densely curled hair which
hung in ringlets around her face. Mutio had darkened
and arched her eyebrows and rendered subtle changes
to her features, which somehow made her eyes look
bigger and her lips smaller, redder and more pouty.
She looked girlish and innocent, in appearance at least
– but Mutio could do nothing to temper the steely
forcefulness of her personality. 'Well?' she demanded.
'Now we're all dolled up, we might as well have a plan.'

'What about trying to find Gaius Canio again?'
suggested Lucius.

'That kid did nothing for us,' said Quin dismissively.
'He knew all about the law and nothing about the
real world – let himself get completely outfoxed by
Glabrio. He even managed to lose those papers we'd
travelled half the world to find. I say we're better off
without him.'

Lucius found it hard to disagree with much of this
– though he wouldn't have put it quite so harshly.
'It wasn't totally Gaius's fault that we lost that court
battle,' he said. 'He did warn us that we needed
another piece of clinching evidence, which we might
have found if we'd had a bit more time. I accept that
Gaius ultimately failed us, but for a while he gave us
real hope. I think we should give him one more chance.
Isi, what do you think?'

She shrugged, and he could see immediately from

her face that, for once, she was inclined to agree with Quin. She'd never been very enthusiastic about their chances of a legal victory against Glabrio anyway. In terms of his belief in Gaius, Lucius was on his own.

It irritated him slightly that the others weren't offering any practical alternatives, though, so he decided to list and dismiss them himself. 'Look,' he said, 'we've already decided that assassinating Glabrio in the street isn't going to be possible. And we can hardly incite the mob when we daren't even show our real faces on the streets. So our only hope is the legal route. And Gaius is the only lawyer we know… He always said we needed some other evidence besides the autopsy report. Well, maybe that woman Val mentioned – the one who witnessed Glabrio ordering the priest to poison Titus's food – maybe she'll provide us with that evidence.'

'I don't think Aleta will help us,' said Val. 'She got so frightened when I asked her if she would.'

'It's pointless anyway, as we no longer have the autopsy report,' said Quin with a frustrated thump of his fist against the wall.

Lucius looked down. He dug his thumbnail into the rough grain of the table surface. 'We have to keep going,' he said bleakly. 'What other choice do we have?'

CHAPTER XI

15–16 SEPTEMBER

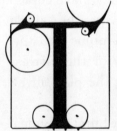

They found Gaius in the Forum, near the steps of the Temple of Castor and Pollux, in an area set aside for civil and criminal trials. Gaius was remonstrating before a magistrate, and for a moment they assumed that he was on trial. But then they saw the shabby, morose-looking figure standing behind him, and they realised that he was acting as this person's defence lawyer.

Lucius led the others closer, pushing his way through the watching crowd to obtain a better view. Praetorian Guardsmen were on duty nearby in their shiny armour and handsome white-plumed helmets – but Lucius felt secure in his new face, and didn't hesitate to show it. He'd secreted a small fruit knife belonging to Faustina in a compartment in the sole of his sandal – he'd once hidden a tiny pugio[*] there in a failed attempt to kill Glabrio. The fruit knife wasn't as sharp as the pugio, but it gave him a degree of confidence knowing he'd be able to defend himself against sudden attack.

'As all professional bakers are aware,' Gaius was saying in his high-pitched voice, 'there are so many variables in the process of baking bread that it is well nigh impossible to produce a loaf of consistent weight. There are variations in the wheat, the flour, the heat of the oven and so on.' As he spoke, he made dramatic flourishes with his arms in a style he must have copied from watching senators giving great speeches about the state of the empire. 'My client, Dubius Crustus, is an honest man, and deeply sorry for the distress he has caused by accidentally selling the plaintiff an underweight loaf.'

Gaius had to raise his voice above the burst of cynical laughter this statement elicited from the watching crowd. 'He has sworn to make it up to her by offering her three loaves absolutely free,' Gaius squeaked. He gestured behind him at the sullen-looking defendant. 'As you can see, my client has been made thoroughly miserable by this whole affair and begs humbly for the forgiveness of the plaintiff and the court and wishes only for the opportunity to continue plying his modest trade without harassment.'

[*] *pugio: a soldier's dagger.*

The hooknosed magistrate did not look impressed. 'Nice try, young Canio,' he said, 'but in my role as aedile of this city, in charge of quality control, I've come across Dubius Crustus before. Now what was it last time? Ah yes, hiding bits of metal in the dough to give it extra weight, that was it.'

'But–' Gaius began, before getting drowned out by angry shouts from the crowd.

'He always hides the underweight loaves at the back of the shelf and takes them out after the inspectors have been,' someone called out.

'I've heard he soaks stale bread in water and mixes it with new dough,' bellowed someone else.

'That would explain the disgusting taste of his bread,' shouted a woman, to general laughter and applause.

The magistrate banged his gavel impatiently. 'Court orders the defendant to pay the plaintiff damages to the value of ten denarii.* And he can consider himself very lucky not to be charged with a criminal offence this time. Case dismissed!'

As Gaius walked disconsolately away, Lucius grabbed his arm. He jerked it away. 'I'm just his lawyer,' he cried bitterly. 'I didn't bake the bread. Now leave me be.'

'Gaius!' hissed Lucius. 'It's me! Lucius!'

Gaius jumped in surprise. He looked up, and squinted at Lucius's face. 'Lucius?' he queried.

* ten denarii: equivalent to ten days' wages for an ordinary labourer.

'Sssh!' whispered Lucius with a quick glance towards the Praetorians.

'B-but you look completely different,' stammered Gaius. 'Your eyes, your hair. What's happened to you?'

'We're in disguise,' said Quin, making Gaius jump even higher.

'Q-Q-Quin?'

His gaze widened to take in the others. 'By the gods, and you must be Isi. And...'

'Valeria,' said Val, stepping forward.

'Sergius.'

'Faustina.'

'What happened to you?' asked Gaius, turning again to Lucius. 'I mean, I heard about the break-out from the ludus, and I hoped... But then I didn't hear any more and I just assumed you'd been captured or killed.'

'We've been on the run, Gaius,' said Lucius. 'We wanted to find you to let you know we were OK and to... to ask you what you thought about filing a lawsuit against Glabrio, as we originally intended. I mean, I know there's probably no hope but...'

Gaius's mouth dropped open.

'Of course there's no hope,' said Quin. 'It was a ridiculous idea even coming here. Not my idea, I should add. You've clearly moved on in your career, Gaius. We're sorry to have wasted your time. Come on, guys, let's get out of here.' He began heading back across the Forum.

'No, Quin, wait!' shouted Gaius. 'Come back here.'

Quin turned, frowning. 'What is it?'

Gaius jerked his thumb over his shoulder towards the open-air law court. 'That's not a career, it's a daily humiliation. Until I acquire a reputation, I'll never attract a case I can win, and until I attract a case I can win, I'll never acquire a reputation. It's an impossible situation.'

'Maybe we can offer you a case you can win,' said Sergius.

Isi smiled. 'And after that, maybe we can offer you the sun, the moon and the stars. What case exactly, Sergius? We haven't got a case.'

'Maybe you have,' said Gaius quietly. 'Maybe you have.'

'What do you mean?' asked Lucius, suddenly alert.

'Follow me,' said the lawyer mysteriously. 'Let's go and find somewhere a little less public. Then I'll tell you everything.'

Gaius shepherded them out of the Forum and down a winding back street to a tiny popina* on the ground floor of a narrow tenement. The windows were dark, and all that identified it as an eaterie was a sign hanging above the door depicting a steaming bowl of stew surrounded by bread and olives. 'I sometimes meet clients here for a private chat,' said Gaius, as he ushered them through the door. A fat man wearing a grease-stained tunic stood behind the counter. His

* popina: a wine bar selling fast food.

multiple chins were flecked with grey stubble. One or two customers sat on stools at the tables provided, nursing their cups. There was a smell of sawdust and rough wine.

'Are there tables available at the back, Gemellus?' Gaius asked the barman.

'Help yourself,' grunted Gemellus.

Gaius turned to the others. 'Hungry, anyone? I can recommend the stew.'

Seven bowls of stew were ordered, and they filed past the counter to a back room, where more customers could be found, crouched in the shadows over small tables, drinking and talking. Lucius heard low laughter and the click of dice being rolled. Light from the wall-torches gleamed on greasy skin and gold teeth.

'So this is where you find your clients?' Quin said sardonically.

'I don't have much choice,' said Gaius. 'The classier types aren't interested in hiring my services – not yet, anyway. But maybe my luck is about to change. And maybe yours as well. Let's find a place to sit.' They moved a few empty tables together and gathered around them on stools.

'What do you mean?' asked Lucius.

Gaius leaned in towards them, and hunched his shoulders conspiratorially. Instinctively, everyone moved closer to hear what he had to say. 'The political winds are changing,' he said in a low voice. 'Let's just say that Glabrio isn't quite as secure in his position as he once was. His systematic murder of political enemies and appropriation of their properties has attracted a whispering campaign against him in the court of Domitian. No one's openly spoken out against him yet – the emperor's advisors are all still terrified of him and no one is prepared to make the first move. But you can be sure that as soon as someone does, they'll all be queueing up to stick the knife in. But that someone will probably have to be an outsider.' He gave Lucius a meaningful stare.

Lucius, profoundly encouraged by all this, blurted: 'You mean us? The lawsuit?'

'A lawsuit against Glabrio could be enough to start the process of ending his reign of terror,' nodded Gaius. 'It's common knowledge that Glabrio bribed witnesses in the first trial. If we could get them back again to testify – people like Vedrix and Mikon and Pavo – and persuade them to tell the truth this time, we could create the necessary momentum for a tidal shift against Glabrio.'

'It's not enough,' said Quin. 'Whatever those fellows say, it won't threaten Glabrio in the slightest. We need the autopsy report for that, and that's been destroyed.'

'Who says it's been destroyed?' said Gaius, a crafty smile playing on his cherubic lips.

Now he really had their attention.

Gaius chuckled at their gaping faces. 'What? You think I handed over the original documents to

Glabrio's cronies? Of course I knew they'd force me to hand them over, so I spent the whole night before the trial copying them out, and I handed them the copies. The originals are still safely hidden in that drainage tunnel by Lake Albano.'

Hearing this, Lucius very nearly let out a whoop of joy, constrained only by the need not to attract attention. Instead, he reached over and squeezed Gaius's shoulder, smiling gleefully at him. Clever, clever Gaius! Somehow just being with him gave Lucius a lift, and he knew now that his instincts had been right in seeking him out. The young lawyer might be inexperienced, but he was intelligent and resourceful and, most important, he was on their side.

The stew arrived, and they all tucked in. Lucius was pleased to see that even Isi was looking more cheerful now. She glanced up and noticed him looking at her from across the table. Lucius looked away, embarrassed for some reason. Then he felt her hand on his. He looked at her and saw she was smiling, but also a little sad. 'I'm sorry,' she whispered. 'You were right, I was wrong. This was exactly the right thing to do.' Their hands joined, and Lucius felt a thrill of warm delight that almost made him giddy.

Meanwhile, a perplexed Quin was still trying to make sense of what Gaius had just said about the documents. 'Why did you lie to us before?' he asked.

'I couldn't risk telling you the truth,' Gaius replied. 'You might have given away the information under torture. I'm sorry, my friends, but those documents are more important than any individual lives – yours or mine – they're the only evidence anyone's found that actually connects Glabrio to the murder of Titus.'

'Not quite the only evidence,' said Isi. 'There's this slave woman…'

They told Gaius about Aleta, and his face broke into a smile of such dazzling hope, it lifted everyone's spirits still higher.

'We must get hold of her,' he said with quiet intensity. 'She is the key to everything.'

Now they all turned to Val.

'She definitely won't come willingly,' she warned them.

'Then we'll kidnap her,' said Quin.

'Does she ever go out?' Isi asked.

Val nodded. 'She's at the meat market at the Forum Boarium each day at noon. But please… Be gentle with her.'

The following day at noon, they entered the crowded market of the Forum Boarium. Lucius, Quin, Isi, Valeria and Sergius were there – Faustina had decided not to join them on this expedition. They entered boldly, with their faces fully exposed. Mutio had given them tips and sold them the tools and materials to do the necessary maintenance on their disguises each morning, so discretion wasn't necessary. They breathed the rich, salty, blood smell coming off the stalls where leather-aproned men displayed their glistening carcasses. This was the city's meat and fish market. In the cracks of the cobbles, blood pooled. Baskets were heaped with silver flesh freshly scooped from the sea. Dead, milk-white eyes stared up at them as they passed.

'Tell us when you see her, Val,' said Quin, looking gaunt and pale as a corpse in his make-up.

Val's freshly rouged cheeks flushed an even deeper red as she scanned the multitude. 'There are so many people,' she despaired. 'I can't… Wait!' Her eyes widened and she darted towards a throng of customers queueing up at a stall where rows of plucked, headless chickens hung from hooks. 'That's her!' she half-cried, half-whispered, pointing at an elderly lady in a long black stola with her head covered in a shawl. She was in the thickest part of the queue.

'OK, well done, Val,' said Isi. 'Now, let's plan this carefully. We mustn't do anything that might alarm her…'

But Quin was already on the move, snaking his way through the swarms of people and plunging into the pack of poultry purchasers.

Lucius watched, transfixed and appalled, as Quin elbowed aside the people around Aleta and blatantly grabbed the old lady around her middle, before hauling

her up and out of the crowd. Aleta didn't go meekly
or quietly. She screamed and kicked and cursed and
began whacking Quin hard on the back with her small
fists. Quin was laughing as he manhandled her away,
and perhaps this response angered and emboldened
the people nearby, because a number of customers
began beating him with their sticks and shopping
bags. Quin stumbled as he tried to get away from
them. Clutching his outraged victim with one arm, he
clambered back to his feet and swung around to face
his attackers. Aleta was by now pulling at his hair and
twisting his ear, making him roar with anger and pain.
He began clobbering his attackers with his spare fist
until they backed off. Then he careered dizzily away
from the market square, with Aleta under his arm, and
disappeared down an alley.

Isi watched all this with her hands clutched to her
face in wide-eyed disbelief. Val looked on the verge of
tears, while Sergius fixed his gaze on the cloud-filled
sky. 'It's starting to rain,' he muttered.

'C'mon,' said Lucius to his stupefied companions.
'Let's get after him.'

They found Quin in a narrow passageway between
two buildings, twenty paces down the alley. He was
scowling and clutching his forearm. Aleta was slumped
in an unconscious heap at his feet.

'What did you do to her?' Val screamed at him. She
dropped to a crouch and put a tender hand to the old
lady's cheek.

'The vicious hag bit me on the arm,' said Quin. 'I had to slap her.'

'You are a complete idiot,' Isi said to him, enunciating every syllable with cold precision, like a teacher talking to an impetuous schoolboy. 'You don't ever *think*, do you? You just wade in and expect everything to go your way.'

Quin looked hurt by this remark. 'I got her, didn't I?'

'You nearly *killed* her,' said Isi. '*And* you attracted the attention of half the marketplace. We were trying to be discreet – and you almost provoked a riot.'

'How is she?' asked Lucius.

'She's opening her eyes,' said Val. The woman was blinking slowly, looking dazed. There was a red mark on her cheek where Quin had clouted her.

'Aleta,' said Val softly. 'Aleta, it's me, Valeria.'

'Mistress?' she muttered vaguely. 'Am I dreaming?' Then her eyes shot open. 'Mistress Valeria!' she cried. 'Oh, gods! What happened to you? Your hair! Your face!'

Val laughed through her tears. 'It's a disguise, Aleta.'

The old lady touched her bruised cheek and moaned. 'I've been attacked! I've been assaulted!' She flinched as she caught sight of Quin standing over her. 'Monstrous, monstrous man! May you rot in Hades.' She stared up at him with a mixture of fear and outrage.

'The rain's getting heavier,' remarked Sergius.

Lucius could feel wet splashes on his cheeks.

'It's OK, Aleta!' soothed Val. 'He's my brother. He didn't mean to hurt you. I'm so sorry, but we had to get you away from the market.'

'Your brother? The one who died and then came back to life?'

Val nodded. 'And there's Lucius, my other brother. And these two are our friends, Isidora and Sergius.'

Aleta eyed them all with deep suspicion. Then she suddenly gripped Val's arm. 'Mistress, you must come home at once. Your mother is beside herself with worry. Why did you run away? Was it to be with your brothers? Don't you know they are both dangerous criminals?'

Val gently detached herself from Aleta's clawlike grip. 'I'm not going back there,' she said. 'You know what Glabrio is – what he did. You told me so yourself.'

'But your mother–'

'She is not my mother,' said Val quietly but firmly. 'Not any more. That woman is every inch as evil as Glabrio. She knew he planned to kill the emperor. She even…' Val choked on her words, and for a moment was unable to continue. Lucius put a comforting hand on her shoulder. She turned to him. Her face shone like the moon in the pearly light of the raincloud. 'She conspired in the murder of our father,' said Val, her gaze still fixed on Lucius. He saw she was trembling. There were desperate creases in her forehead.

'We don't know that,' said Quin.

Val hooded her eyes and her face became a mask. 'That night, she went to Glabrio and told him to kill our father. We can tell ourselves otherwise, but I'm certain that's what happened.' To Aleta, she said: 'My brothers are not criminals. They're just trying to avenge the death of our father, and to save our family from that monster Glabrio... But to do that, they – we – need your help.'

'No, mistress.' Aleta tried to scramble to her feet, but Val placed a restraining hand on her shoulder.

'You must tell the people in the court what you saw that day last year – when you saw Glabrio tell the cook to poison the emperor's food.'

Aleta burst into tears. 'No, mistress. I cannot do it. I don't care about myself. I don't care if I die. But I have a daughter, and a grandson. I'm scared he will kill them. Please don't make me do this.'

Val, dismayed by these words, released her. Aleta struggled to her feet, still sobbing, and began making her way back up the alley.

Halfway down, she turned. 'Shall I... shall I tell your mother you're alive, mistress?' she asked.

'No,' said Val. 'Don't tell her or anyone else that you've seen us.'

The old slave nodded and continued on her way.

'If you help us,' Isi called after her retreating figure, 'you'll have nothing to fear from Glabrio, because he'll be destroyed. He won't be able to hurt you or your family!'

She had to shout these last words, because Aleta had increased her speed to get away. In despondent silence, they watched her disappear through a hazy curtain of rain into the light and bustle of the forum.

'It's getting quite wet now,' commented Sergius.

'Your make-up –' Isi said to Val. 'It's running.'

'Curses!' said Quin. 'We're losing our disguises.'

As he said this, the view ahead was darkened by the silhouettes of a horde of helmeted figures, and the alley echoed to a hailstorm of iron-soled feet.

How? Lucius wanted to cry. *How did they know we were here? It was Hector. It had to be Hector...*

'Run!' Quin shouted at Val.

'No!' she screamed. 'I'm staying with you. Together forever, remember? You're not going to abandon me again!'

Grim-faced Praetorians were hurtling towards them, four abreast between the close walls of the alley. The first ones would be upon them in a heartbeat.

'Sergius!' bellowed Quin. 'Get Val out of here. Take her back to Faustina's. We'll try and hold them up for as long as we can.'

Sergius nodded and dragged Val away. The last Lucius saw of her, she had her eyes closed and her mouth open wide in a shriek of 'NO!' The rain, which was pelting down now, had smeared her make-up and turned her wig into a tangled mess. Lucius clenched his jaw and tried to close his mind to the sight. Turning away from her, he was in time to witness his brother charging headlong into the front rank of the Praetorians. A memory flashed through Lucius's brain of a scene one year earlier to the day, on the Pontine Marshes, when Quin had done exactly the same.

PART FOUR

CARPE DIEM

CHAPTER XII

16–17 SEPTEMBER

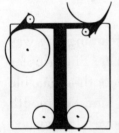he battle in the alley was over in seconds – after a dizzying blow to the head, Lucius found himself face down in a gutter gushing with filthy rainwater, a sword tip threatening to bury itself in the back of his neck. Just before he fell, he glimpsed Isi surrounded, bent double after a punch to the stomach. Nearby, he could hear Quin struggling on for a short while longer before he, too, was clouted into submission. A gruff, plebeian[*] voice barked an order: 'Two got away in the direction of the river. After them!'

Lucius suddenly rolled clear of the sword and kicked out, connecting with a shin. A soldier yelped. Before

[*] *plebeian: working-class.*

anyone could react, Lucius was on his feet, barging into another Praetorian and clunking him on the helmet. *Anything to delay them*, he thought, deliriously.

His act of reckless defiance might or might not have bought Sergius and Valeria a few more precious seconds – all it bought Lucius was a choking neck lock followed by a hard punch to the jaw. He dropped to his knees, watching the blood dribble from his face and join the torrent flowing down the street. Another blow, this time from the flat of a gladius, came down on his unprotected skull, and the world went dark.

A long time later, he found himself dreaming. He was looking up into the face of his mother. Soft ripples of light shimmered across her smooth-as-marble features. She was speaking gently to him, her mouth barely moving. Were they words of love? He wished he could hear what she was saying. From somewhere nearby came the tinkling echo of falling water. He could feel the coolness of a perfumed sponge being dabbed on his face. Was she washing him? It felt nice. He wanted to tell her: *Mother, I've heard terrible things about you. Things you knew about. Plots you were involved in...* But he was scared – in case she confirmed it was all true. He wanted to go on feeling safe – for a while longer, at least – here in her care.

Gradually, his senses returned. Pain throbbed in

his head, the hazy veil across his vision lifted and he saw the hard ice at the centre of her blue-eyed stare. He registered the sternness of her mouth, the grating insistence of her voice. 'Where is she, Lucius? What have you done with her?'

He wasn't dreaming. And she didn't love him – not any more.

'Mother,' he said, his voice barely a whisper.

'Stop fussing over him, Caecilia,' came a shrill, nasal voice that cut through the atmosphere like an aggressively flung pilum.* 'Valeria will be found. It's only a question of time.'

Caecilia immediately dropped the sponge she'd been holding and stood up. Lucius tried to rise, and only then discovered he was shackled at the wrists by heavy iron bracelets. Using his elbows, he managed to lift himself into a seated position. He was on a cushion-softened marble seat in an enormous atrium. On the distant walls were faint frescoes showing chubby infants busy with various trades, such as wine-making, minting coins and perfume-pressing. Rain dripped and drizzled from the opening in the roof high above into the large impluvium next to where he sat.

Standing in the centre of the room, an immaculate toga draped over his lean frame, was the hawk-nosed, skull-faced Glabrio. One hand was laid casually on his hip, and the forefinger of the other hand gently rubbed his chin as he contemplated Lucius. To his left

* pilum: a Roman soldier's spear.

stood the grey-haired, smiling praetor whom Lucius recalled from the trial. Lucius felt no reassurance from the man's benign, avuncular appearance. He was Glabrio's creature, like everyone else. What else could explain his presence here in Glabrio's domus?* Also close by were half a dozen Praetorian Guardsmen in bright red cloaks and highly polished armour. They surrounded the figures of Quin and Isi, who were, like Lucius, shackled by the wrists.

So here they all were in the monster's lair, utterly at his mercy. In their quest to defeat him, they'd tried to capture Aleta, and ended up getting captured themselves!

'You young idiots,' said Glabrio, the sweep of his gaze taking in Lucius, Quin and Isi. 'You've had some dumb luck, I'll admit, escaping execution and then taking advantage of that breakout from the ludus – but did you really expect I wouldn't catch up with you in the end?'

His voice whined and wheedled like an unpleasant buzzing insect. He looked like an old, sun-shrivelled lizard, with all the love and humanity squeezed out of him. His eyes, beneath their hooded lids, seemed to assess things rather than see them, as if the world were simply an assortment of objects for him to either possess or dispose of.

'You are so misguided,' he said to Lucius and Quin. 'So twisted with fear and malice. Just like your late father–'

_____
* _domus: town house._

'Murderer!' screamed Quin.

A guard moved to strike him for this insolence, but Glabrio merely smiled and inclined his head in a magnanimous gesture. 'Let the fool have his say. Pray tell, Quintus Valerius, whom you think I have murdered?'

'The emperor Titus!' said Quin.

This didn't provoke the shockwave of anger that Lucius had expected or hoped for. Instead, Caecilia's face remained a mask; the praetor frowned slightly, but said nothing; and Glabrio's thin lips merely spread into a rictus-like smile. 'Just like your father,' he said. 'He, too, was a fantasist of the first order who saw conspiracy and subterfuge when the truth was far more straightforward. Titus died of a fever. Boring, I know, but that's all there is to it.'

Lucius felt physically weak, but anger at this lie seemed to sharpen his mind, and drove him to challenge Glabrio: 'Then why did the physician who examined the emperor's body conclude that he'd been poisoned?' he asked.

'He didn't,' said Glabrio calmly. 'His autopsy report clearly states–'

'The autopsy report that you forced him to change,' interrupted Lucius. 'We've seen the original.'

The praetor's frown deepened a few notches at this, but again he remained silent.

'I don't know what you've seen,' said Glabrio, 'but whatever it was, it wasn't the autopsy report. There was only one such report and it stated that Titus died of a fever.'

Lucius lapsed into silence, realising there was no point in pursuing the argument. He certainly wasn't going to tell Glabrio or the praetor that the original autopsy report still existed – better to let them believe they'd destroyed it. That way, if Gaius ever did manage to file his lawsuit, they would be in for a surprise.

Glabrio continued: 'It was a shame that your father, who loved Titus as much as he feared Domitian, decided to concoct his own version of events. He wanted to destroy me, just as he destroyed his brother – but fate prevented it.'

'You mean *you* prevented it by murdering him!' bellowed Quin. Then he vented his fury on Caecilia. 'And you, *Mother!* – you connived at Father's murder. You fled here that night a year ago, and told Glabrio that Father planned to expose the regicide in a speech to the Senate the next day. Then the two of you sent that assassin, Eprius, to our house. Admit it!'

'How dare you!' Caecilia breathed, turning pale. 'You evil, evil boy. To think that I once loved you as my son… I suppose you've told these malicious lies to Valeria.'

'We told her *everything*, and you should know that she hates you!'

Caecilia stiffened. Her hands, Lucius saw, were shaking.

Glabrio, however, maintained an unruffled air.

'Aquila may be dead,' he smiled, 'but it's amusing to
see that his spirit lives on in his sons – for now, at least.
But you two are still damnati ad gladium, let's not
forget, and your recent escape from the ludus doesn't
change that – if anything, it will make things worse
for you.'

'How could things be any worse?' muttered Quin.

'Oh, let me see,' said Glabrio, tapping his chin and
pretending to give the matter some thought. 'How
about... this time we make you fight without armour
or weapons!'

His smile betrayed his own sick amusement at the
idea: no chance to defend themselves. Their flesh and
nothing more – against sharpened steel.

'You can't do that!' shouted Quin.

'I can, and I will,' replied the consul. He nodded at
Isi. 'And your accomplice will share the same fate.'

'Um...' The praetor cleared his throat. 'Strictly
speaking, my friend, the boy is right. The court must
decide on punishments...'

Glabrio turned and directed his gaze at the praetor.
'Are you saying I'm exceeding my authority, Marius?'

The praetor's fleshy jaw trembled. 'I'm, uh, afraid
so. Sentencing has to be by the courts. And the girl –
the g-girl has not even been tried yet.'

'I see,' said Glabrio quietly, and he opened out a
thin, bony hand to ponder his nails. Then the hand
closed into a fist and he whirled around and punched
the praetor hard in the stomach.

The praetor uttered a low, breathy groan and bent forward as if grovelling before his master. Glabrio grabbed the back of his neck and shoved him hard to the floor, where his forehead made an audible clunk on contact with the marble.

Lucius felt the saliva dry from his open mouth. *He's an old man*, he thought. *A dignified man. He was simply stating a legal truth.*

'Never defy me again, Marius,' said Glabrio with almost supernatural calm. 'Do you understand?'

The praetor coughed and nodded. He rubbed his forehead.

'Do you understand?' shrieked Glabrio.

'Yes,' said the praetor quickly.

This is a senator, thought Lucius. *A learned man. A magistrate. Being treated like an errant slave.*

The praetor began to get to his feet, but Glabrio shoved him back down onto his knees. 'Did I tell you you could get up yet? Did I?!'

'N-no.'

'Now beg for forgiveness.'

'What?' The praetor looked up, his mouth a perfect 'O' of shock.

'Beg for forgiveness.'

'Marcus, this is too much,' pleaded the praetor. 'I'm your colleague, your friend, I… I've been loyal…'

'Beg, you snivelling wretch. Or you'll never see your wife and children again. Not alive, at any rate.'

The praetor emitted a choking sound. His face

had gone almost as grey as his hair. 'I-I... beg your forgiveness,' he whimpered.

Glabrio stared stonily at the man at his feet. Then his lips broke open in a smile. His eyes crinkled with amusement, and he began to laugh. He reached down and helped the praetor to his feet. 'Marius! My dear old friend!' he giggled, embracing him. The praetor wiped his eyes, trying hard not to cry. On his forehead was a red mark that would soon become a bruise.

Soon afterwards, the guards led Lucius, Quin and Isi away. Lucius cast a final glance at Caecilia. She hadn't reacted at all to her husband-to-be's humiliation of the praetor. Perhaps she'd witnessed that sort of scene too often before to be affected by it. Or perhaps her worship of power was so great that she'd lost all moral sensibility. Her eyes were hard as she watched her sons leave the room – there was no love, pity or regret in them; it was as though the shutters were closed. The boys were nothing to her now.

It was noon on the thirteenth day of the Roman Games at the Flavian Amphitheatre – almost time for the prisoner executions. Usually, this was the cue for a mass exodus from the amphitheatre as the hungry crowds descended on the fast-food stalls that lined the concourse outside. But today was different: the seats remained almost three-quarters full. Hastily painted signs had appeared that morning on walls around the city, and they had stirred considerable interest among afficionados of the games. The signs read:

Today at sexta hora:[*] Execution of convicted criminals. For the amusement of the lunchtime crowds, the prisoners will not be tied up today, nor fed to wild beasts. They will be allowed the freedom of the arena. They can run. They can even fight back, should they wish. But they won't have armour or weapons – unlike their executioners, who will be veteran gladiators. Three prisoners versus three gladiators. Sounds interesting, doesn't it? How long will the prisoners last? Don't miss out on the fun!

To add to the excitement, a rumour had spread that morning that the prisoners in question were none other than the Phoenix of Pompeii and his brother Lucius, who'd been recaptured following their now-famous escape from the Ludus Romanus. With them, so the gossip went, was an accomplice who'd helped break them out of the ludus. The rumour, which had begun in the Forum Boarium and quickly spread all the way to Suburra, had attracted a crowd of quite astounding proportions to the concourse outside the amphitheatre. There were blacksmiths, weaponsmiths, taverners, cobblers, butchers, fishmongers, bakers, hairdressers and fullers,[**] many of them there with their wives, children and slaves. None had tickets for

[*] *sexta hora: the sixth hour of the day, i.e. noon.*
[**] *fullers: laundry workers.*

the day's games, yet all were planning to make as much noise and show as much appreciation for their heroes as they possibly could.

Meanwhile, the three heroes were in a heavily guarded cell in the Ludus Romanus on the far side of the concourse. Unaware of what was happening outside, they were busy trying to work out a strategy for what they would do once they were inside the arena.

'On no account should we run away from the gladiators or let them split us up,' said Quin, pacing the room. 'We must stand or fall together. The plan will depend on perfect timing, and not all getting attacked at once.'

'It's not going to work,' said Isi, who was seated on the floor, leaning back against the wall, her eyes half closed. 'However quick we are, they'll have armour and weapons, and we won't. That's all there is to it.'

'We've got to stay positive!' Quin shouted at her. 'Or do you want us to just show them our necks like a bunch of sacrificial bullocks?'

Isi opened her eyes fully. 'No,' she said. 'I want to survive – which is why I think that trying to attack them is the worst possible idea. Surely it's better to split up and run. We won't be weighed down like them. We can wear them out.'

'I've never run away from anyone,' growled Quin.

GLADIATOR SCHOOL

'Great!' muttered Isi sarcastically. 'So we must all sacrifice ourselves on the altar of Quin's pride.'

They'll be bickering to the end, thought Lucius miserably. He still had a headache from the blow to his head. He'd had a terrible night, having been kept awake by an irregular clanging sound that had seemed to emanate from the walls and floor – perhaps it had been in his head. And now the sole of his left foot was feeling sore. He removed his sandal, and something dropped with a clatter to the floor – something small and sharp. He'd forgotten all about the fruit knife he'd hidden in there. So that was what had caused the discomfort! He held it up to the others. 'Perhaps we do have a slight chance,' he grinned.

Quin's face lit up at the sight of it.

There came a sudden clatter of footsteps and a rattle of keys at the cell door. Lucius hurriedly returned the knife to its little compartment and replaced the sandal on his foot.

Several guards entered the cell, followed, unexpectedly, by the short, stocky figure of Appius Seius Crassus, the school's lanista.

'To what do we owe this honour, Crassus?' asked Quin, smiling grimly.

Crassus didn't reply. He looked older somehow. His steely eyes were red-rimmed, and his craggy face seemed carved from something a little softer than the usual granite. Perhaps the mass breakout had shaken him – perhaps he was being replaced.

'Where's Hector?' he asked them. It was possibly the last question Lucius had expected.

'I know he escaped with you fellows. But he's not been seen or heard of since.'

He stared fiercely at them, willing them to answer.

'We don't know,' said Lucius eventually. 'He ran away from the place where we were hiding.'

'I need him back,' said Crassus. 'I… I had plans for him. Where do you think he went?'

'You don't want to have anything more to do with that maniac,' said Quin.

'What are you talking about?' said Crassus, aghast.

'He killed Hilario,' explained Isi. 'Strangled him in his sleep, then very nearly did the same to Lucius.'

'We thought he might be working for Glabrio,' added Lucius.

Crassus went very still. He almost seemed to stop breathing. Then, very quietly, he said: 'You're mistaken. Hector would never kill anyone in their sleep. And he doesn't *work* for anyone, except me.' He let out a hiss of breath. 'I know… I know he can be mouthy sometimes. Thinks a bit too much of himself. But he's basically a good kid. If anything, he's soft. I was working on that side of him. Trying to give him some of that inner steel, like you've got –' He nodded at Quin. 'That's why I made him primus palus…'

'Why bother?' said Quin. 'There were plenty of better fighters, better men, you could have chosen. Hilario, for instance.'

'Because…' Crassus's gaze seemed to turn inwards. He looked more vulnerable, more exposed, than Lucius could ever remember. 'Because,' he said gravely, 'Hector is my son.'

The words hung in the air like a strange echo, as Lucius and the other two struggled to process this new information.

'So that's why you told me to lose that fight against him,' said Quin.

Lucius thought he saw a gleam of moisture in the lanista's eye. 'He doesn't know,' he said softly. 'He thinks he rose through his own merits. If he ever finds out I'm his father, it'll destroy his confidence… I just hope the lad's all right – wherever he is…'

Then he straightened his shoulders and clenched his jaw. 'Boys,' he said to Lucius and Quin. 'Isidora… I don't make speeches, as you know. And I make it a rule never to question the decisions of those in power. But if you want my opinion, for what it's worth, I think this stinks what they're doing to you today. They should at least put swords in your hands. This is a perversion of the whole gladiator ethic. It honours no one, least of all the lads who're going to have to hack you down. There you are. I've said it. It's not good. You deserve better. So all I can say is, go out there and die like Romans.' He glanced at Isi. 'And in case you were wondering, young lady, you're a Roman, too – whether you like it or not.' He gave a nod to the guards, then turned on his heel and departed.

Whether it was Crassus's doing, they never found out, but the three of them were escorted to the amphitheatre, not via the recently built underground tunnel, but the old way: through the front doors of the ludus and across the open-air concourse. As soon as they came out of the ludus, they were confronted by the roar of hundreds of fans. A double cordon of guards had created a pathway for them, leading to the gladiators' entrance of the amphitheatre, but the organisers clearly hadn't anticipated either the size or the enthusiasm of the crowd, and the cordon was threatening to break in several places even before Quin, Lucius and Isi appeared.

It was a stirring sight. Lucius felt overwhelmed as he gazed from the steps of the ludus across the sea of heads cheering and chanting their names. He trembled with a mixture of emotions – astonishment, pride, gratitude, but also sadness that all this support was to be in vain. He read some of the crudely daubed signs held up above people's heads: *Phoenix of Pompeii Forever* – *Lucius We Love You* – *Heroes of the People*. *The New Spartacans* read one sign, a reference to the great slave revolt of a hundred and fifty years earlier, which had also begun with a mass breakout from a gladiator school.

'I can't believe it,' muttered Lucius as the three of

them raised their hands and waved to the crowds.

'This has to be Faustina's doing,' said Isi.

'Or Val's,' said Quin.

They made their way along the narrow, swaying pathway, with arms reaching in from either side, past the shoulders of the guards forming the cordon, as people attempted to touch their heroes. About halfway along, the cordon was broken by a sudden rush of excited fans. The guards struggled to force the crowd back. Then Lucius felt someone grab his elbow. He turned and was astonished to be confronted by the pale, bearded face of the priest of the Lupercal.

'Young man!' he cried, his voice just about audible above the din. 'After you left the cave, I found…'

He was jostled from behind and nearly lost his footing. Guards were trying to drag him away, but he maintained a painfully tight grip on Lucius's elbow.

'What did you find?' screamed Lucius.

'I found a body,' the priest screamed back. He was virtually horizontal now, as the guards were pulling hard at his lower half, trying to haul him away. 'In the well in the chamber, I found the body of the one called Hector! I told you… I told you he didn't run away that night. His neck… was covered in bruises. He–'

At that moment, the priest's grip slipped, and he quickly fell back and disappeared into the forest of people.

His head spinning with this latest shock, Lucius was shoved, along with the others, in through the amphitheatre entrance. 'Did you hear that?' he managed to shout at Quin and Isi as the three of them were frogmarched along a corridor. 'The priest found Hector's body in the well. He'd been strangled.' As he said this, a memory came to him: moments before being attacked that night, he'd heard, in his dream, the sound of a splash.

Quin twisted his head towards Lucius, eyes wide with disbelief. 'So who was the killer if not Hector?'

'Sergius,' said Isi immediately. 'It has to be Sergius. There's no one else it could have been.'

They stared at each other in horror.

Sergius had Val.

CHAPTER XIII

17 SEPTEMBER

efore they could even think about the implications of this, they were shoved back out into daylight. Lucius blinked at the oval sea of glittering white sand stretching out before them, and the tiers of banked seating that rose up on all sides, seemingly all the way to the heavens. How he would have loved to sprout giant legs right now and climb up those tiers like a grand set of steps, then leap over the topmost wall and escape to freedom. He could stomach the idea of dying today, but he couldn't bear to think of what might have happened to Val in the hands of Sergius – Sergius, who had seemed such a pleasant young man. As Eprius had...

Lucius barely heard the cheering. All his thoughts

were now on Val. He wanted desperately to find her, to reassure himself that she was all right, and not dead in a ditch somewhere. She of all of them had to outlive this nightmare. If Val didn't survive, then his life – in fact, this whole world and everything in it – would be rendered utterly meaningless.

'We have to get through this,' he hissed at the other two as they stumbled their way beneath the glaring midday sun toward the centre of the arena. 'We have to win this one – for Val.'

Quin nodded as he raised an arm to acknowledge the cries of *Phoenix*. 'Carpe diem,'* he muttered.

Isi gritted her teeth. 'We do it your way,' she said to Quin. 'Lucius's knife tips the balance.'

'Good girl,' smiled Quin. He whispered the plan to them once again, so they each knew what they had to do. It seemed an almost ludicrously difficult manoeuvre to bring off, depending on incredible speed of movement and split-second timing, as well as a fat dollop of luck – it was imperative that the gladiators didn't all attack at once. The only thing their plan had in its favour was that no one could possibly expect it.

The summa rudis was waiting for them in the middle of the arena. Some way behind him stood their adversaries: a Hoplomachus, a Thraex and a Retiarius. Was this some sort of joke? Did Glabrio mean to humiliate them by forcing each of them to be killed by their own kind? Or had the choice of fighters been

* *Carpe diem: seize the day (i.e. act while you have the chance).*

240

made with a more practical purpose in mind? For these were all parmularii – small-shield fighters. Glabrio must have assumed that Lucius, Quin and Isi would try and run, which might have exhausted a Provocator or Secutor lumbering around with heavy armour and a huge shield – but these fit-looking, lightly armoured young men looked all too eager for the chase. Lucius was now relieved that they'd opted for Quin's plan to stand and fight.

He knew also that fleeing would have been a betrayal of who they were and what they stood for, and would have quickly turned the crowd against them. For now, it seemed, they had the love and respect of at least three-quarters of the paying spectators, as well as countless more gathered on the concourse outside. But that could change… Crassus had been right. If they were to die today, and if their deaths were to mean anything, they should die like Romans, face to face with their killers, and not be hacked down as they fled from them.

Glabrio was seated in the imperial box, surrounded by toga-clad lackeys and uniformed heavies. He didn't look bothered by the support for Quin, Lucius and Isi. In fact, he seemed quietly amused by it. His smile appeared to say: 'I can't stop you loving these miscreants, but you can't stop me killing them either. Tomorrow they'll be gone, but I shall still be here…'

Lucius, incensed by the proud smirk on Glabrio's face, barely listened to the summa rudis as he introduced the event. The man found it hard to make himself heard in any case, above the roar that accompanied his announcement of each of their names.

'Damnati ad gladium!' he concluded. 'Condemned to die by the sword in the arena! According to their sentences, they must fight without weapons and without protection from helmet, shield or armour!'

A great upswelling of jeers and boos followed this pronouncement. 'Give them swords!' came the cries. 'Unfair!' 'Travesty of justice!'

Glabrio smiled on.

The summa rudis called for the fight to begin, and Lucius, Quin and Isi formed themselves into a tight triangle, facing their adversaries. The gladiators advanced on them, the Hoplomachus slightly ahead of the other two. The Hoplomachus and Thraex were big for parmularii, and the scars on their thickly muscled arms and chests bore testimony to their experience. The Retiarius was leaner and had no scars. Unusually, he had opted to join his companions in wearing a face-concealing helmet (Retiarii traditionally fought bare-headed). Lucius wondered if the man had done so to preserve his anonymity, as no self-respecting gladiator would want to be known for hacking down unarmed opponents.

The gladiators were now within ten paces of them, and closing.

'Wait for it,' whispered Quin.

Lucius felt beads of sweat forming on his forehead.

Everything depended on what happened in the next few seconds. If all the gladiators attacked at once, they were done for. If he slipped or fumbled or was just a little slow, they were done for. His muscles were taut as a bowstring. His skin prickled with anticipation. The gladiators were coming within striking distance, the Hoplomachus still in the lead. Good! Hopefully he would strike before the others. But why wasn't Quin giving the signal? Lucius felt himself starting to panic. *Say it, Quin! Give the word!*

The Hoplomachus raised his sword. His target was Quin, at the apex of their triangle.

'Now!' hissed Quin, and Lucius whipped off his sandal and held it before him like a weapon.

The Hoplomachus's arm froze with the sword still high above his head. He uttered a breathless wheeze of laughter, that sounded tinny from within his helmet. There was also some scattered laughter from the spectators, but most were too caught up in the drama to react.

No one saw the tiny knife drop into Lucius's hand.

As the Hoplomachus steadied himself once more to strike at Quin, Lucius flicked the knife. It embedded itself, as he'd intended, in the shoulder of the man's sword arm. The Hoplomachus screamed and dropped the sword.

What followed happened so fast as to appear virtually simultaneous with the knife-flick. Quin darted towards the Thraex, swooping beneath his

slashing blade and diving for the man's legs. The
Thraex tipped forward and, before he could regain his
balance, Lucius kicked upwards at his sword hand,
sending his crescent-shaped sword flying. Isi caught
it in mid-air and whacked it into the shield of the
advancing Retiarius, rocking him backwards. While
Quin knocked the wounded Hoplomachus back onto
the sand, Lucius scooped up his fallen sword. Just in
time he was able to raise this to deflect a blow from the
Retiarius's trident.

It was a manoeuvre that he, Quin and Isi had
practised for hours the night before with imaginary
weapons and opponents (the knife throw had been a
flying kick in their original plan). Yet Lucius couldn't
believe that they'd brought it off so perfectly. A lot,
he realised, was down to its sheer unexpectedness.
No one could have predicted such reckless, all-out
aggression from three people dressed in sandals
and tunics, least of all their armed and armoured
adversaries. The silence that greeted this development
was one of breathless shock – a kind of collective
gasp for air as everyone in the amphitheatre tried to
comprehend what had just happened. The roar that
followed was sheer exultation tinged with disbelief,
and it threatened to blow the entire velarium – the
canvas awning that shaded the crowd from the sun –
right off its moorings.

Yet, down in the furnace of the arena, the fight
was far from over. Lucius and Isi might now have

weapons, but none of them had armour, and the advantages of surprise and momentum were fading fast. The previous night, as he outlined the plan, Quin had never been clear about what they should do next, and as neither Lucius nor Isi believed they would even get *this* far, they hadn't really pressed him on what he had in mind for 'Stage Two'.

Clearly, 'Stage Two' had to involve Quin arming himself by dispossessing the Retiarius of his trident – an implement that no one wielded as well as Quin, save perhaps Neptune himself. But right now, the Retiarius was furiously jabbing the trident at Lucius, while the Hoplomachus was doing the same to Quin with his spear – the fruit knife, it turned out, had not inflicted more than a shallow cut. On the periphery of his vision, Lucius glimpsed Isi locked in a furious fight with the Thraex. She had his sword, but he had a shield, as well as a dagger. She swung the sword against his head, knocking him to his knees. His helmet tumbled off, and Lucius caught sight of a red, sweating, bull-like face.

Lucius refocused on his own fight just in time to deflect a lunging blow towards his stomach. Repeatedly, he clashed his sword against his opponent's trident, trying to break the shaft – but he wasn't used to fighting Retiarii, and the man was adept at keeping the prongs outwards and the shaft protected, no matter what angle Lucius chose to attack from. The Retiarius was quick and alert – he seemed able to predict Lucius's

245

moves, almost as if he'd studied him. And that net he was carrying – it didn't really look like a net at all, now he was at closer quarters with it. More like a….

There was a cry to his right as Isi managed to land a strike, stabbing upwards beneath the Thraex's shield. The man fought on, but blood was now bubbling from between his lips.

The Retiarius took a firmer grip of the thing that wasn't a net, and Lucius saw now that his suspicions were correct: it was a rope. The man flicked it and Lucius felt it snake around his neck. The whirling twine burned his skin and then tightened with sudden, terrifying force. The Laquearius (for that was what he was) yanked at the rope, pulling it taut, and Lucius fell to his knees. He tried to slash with his sword, tried to break the rope, but his arm had no coordination. He needed air. The ocean of sand tipped and swayed, the world warped and stretched. The roar of the crowd deepened to something throbbing and full of menace. Everything slowed. Three sharpened steel points edged closer to his face.

Air! By all the gods, he needed air.

He had his sword up, pressing between the prongs of the trident, using what little strength he had left to keep it from burying itself in his face. He felt himself begin to sink into a softer place. Everything was fading – sun, steel and burning sand, all melting. He could see his father, standing in a sunlit field, waiting for him with open arms. Lucius wanted to run to him. But something was stopping him. Something was holding him back.

A voice:

Lucius. Lucius. Wake up!

He opened his eyes – he hadn't even realised they were closed.

Isi was there, kneeling over him. Her face had blood on it.

'It's over,' she said grimly. 'We won.'

Lucius blinked at her. The tightness around his neck was gone. He could breathe again. On the ground lay the Hoplomachus and the Thraex, both dead. Behind Isi stood Quin. He had a sword in his hand – the Hoplomachus's sword – and he was holding it at the throat of the Laquearius. The Laquearius had lost his helmet. His nose had been smashed, probably by a punch or kick. Somehow Lucius was not surprised to see that it was Sergius.

Sergius the strangler.

Quin was screaming at him: 'Where's Val? What have you done with her?'

Sergius laughed through bloodstained teeth. 'She's hidden,' he said, 'in a secret place that you'll never find. I'd planned to go back there after the fight and kill her. But this is so much better. You'll kill me and then you'll never find her, and she'll slowly starve to death.'

'Why?' Lucius croaked. 'Why are you doing this?'

Sergius didn't reply. He just grabbed the neck of his tunic, gritted his teeth and ripped the garment down the front. The tattoo inscribed on his chest said it all: a kestrel in flight with an arrow through its heart – the symbol of Ravilla, now adopted by all the enemies of Quintus Valerius Aquila and his children.

'Eprius was my friend,' Sergius told Lucius. 'I never told you that, did I? I met him when I was living rough. He told me all about you and your rotten, evil family. But you did inspire me, Lucius. I didn't lie about that. When I watched you kill him, you inspired me to become a gladiator, so I could avenge his death and kill you.'

'Where is our sister?' Quin bawled at him.

Sergius merely smiled. 'She's going to die,' he giggled. 'As will you two when Glabrio gets you. You're all going to die.'

Quin didn't even look towards the imperial box to seek permission for what he did next. If he had, he'd have seen Glabrio's seat vacated in any case. Taking a firmer grip on his sword, he shoved it hard into Sergius's throat, killing him.

Isi cried out: 'But now we'll never–'

The rest of what she had to say was lost in a maelstrom of unbelievable sound that swept through the amphitheatre and carried on outwards like a rising, swirling wind to all the thousands on the concourse outside. It was a joyful, astonished sound, and like nothing Lucius had ever heard before. The spectators were on their feet, laughing and applauding and shouting their heads off. The amazement on their faces seemed to suggest they'd just witnessed a miracle. Perhaps only the appearance of the whole pantheon of gods in their midst would have produced a greater reaction.

Quin helped Lucius to his feet, and the three of them raised their hands in a victory salute. They smiled dutifully, but their smiles were fixed and artificial, for only one question now possessed them: where was Val?

There was no protocol for what should happen next. Prisoner executions were not supposed to conclude with the prisoners still alive and the executioners dead at their feet. And with the crowd in their current mood, it would have taken a very brave games organiser to order a second set of executioners into the arena. Instead, a dozen guards were eventually ordered on and (to a savage chorus of boos and whistles) they proceeded to shackle Lucius, Quin and Isi before escorting them back to the ludus.

They weren't taken to their cell, however, but were delivered instead to Crassus's office next to the quad. Crassus was on his feet waiting for them when they came in. He was actually smiling – an expression Lucius couldn't remember ever having seen adorning the lanista's rugged face. It was a little unnerving.

Crassus dismissed the guards and closed the door,

so they were alone. 'Sergius killed Hilario, right?' he said.

'How could you know that?' blurted Quin.

'Process of deduction,' said Crassus. 'It was only you three, Hector, Hilario and Sergius who escaped together, right? So, assuming you three didn't kill Hilario, it had to be Sergius. I'm right, aren't I? Which means Hector didn't do it. He's innocent.'

'Lanista—' began Lucius.

'I saw you talking to him at the end there,' Crassus blithely went on. 'And then you killed him without even waiting for permission. You were taking revenge for Hilario. I'm right, aren't I? He killed Hilario. Strangled him, just like he nearly strangled you, Lucius.'

Crassus seemed so carried away by his brilliant detective work that he didn't even pause to let the others confirm or deny his conclusions.

'I told you Hector was innocent, didn't I? I told you he'd never kill anyone in cold blood. Now all we've got to do is find him. And I want to enlist your help.'

'Crassus,' said Quin. 'I'm sorry to have to tell you this, but... Hector is dead.'

The smile remained fixed on Crassus's face. It was almost as if, having discovered this new expression, he didn't know how to rid himself of it.

'What?' he said vaguely, as if he'd misheard.

'Hector is dead,' repeated Quin. 'Sergius killed him.'

At last the smile faded. 'No,' said Crassus quietly.

'That cannot be. He's missing, that's all.'

'His body was found by a priest,' said Lucius. 'He'd been strangled, like Hilario.'

Crassus sank into his seat. His lips moved for a while, but he didn't speak. He looked old, Lucius thought. The ageless, unchanging Crassus looked old. And tired.

'I blame myself,' he said eventually. 'I walked out on him and his mother when he was young, maybe only five or six. If I'd been a proper father to him, he'd have developed better. I wanted to make it up to him. In secret, like. Not ever letting him know who I was. I thought, by giving him the right encouragement, I could make up for all those lost years. I could help him make something of himself... Maybe I was a fool to think that, but I'd have done anything for that boy. I can't... I don't want to imagine what it must have been like for him, right at the end, knowing he died a failure.' He paused to wipe an eye. 'Now I wish I'd told him the truth. I'd have told him it didn't matter what he was. He could have been a farmer for all I cared, so long as he knew he had a father who loved him. It was my own stupid pride that made me think he could be a gladiator and kept on thinking that even when it was clear he'd only ever be a second-rate one. He should have been a farmer. Then none of this would have happened...'

'Lanista,' said Lucius as gently as he could. 'We have a favour to ask of you.' He was sorry for Crassus, but his son was dead – nothing could be done for him now. Val was still alive, however. Somehow, they had to negotiate a temporary release so they could get out there and search for her.

Crassus raised his head. 'You killed my son's killer,' he said to them. 'I owe you your freedom.'

They stared back at him, stupefied. 'You can do that?' said Quin. 'You can release us?'

'Not officially, no,' said Crassus. 'You're Glabrio's property officially. But mistakes happen. People escape.'

They didn't move, still incredulous at what the lanista was suggesting.

'If you're going to escape, you'd better do it now,' Crassus prompted. He took a key off the wall behind his desk and began unlocking their shackles. 'Most of the gladiators are in the amphitheatre this afternoon, either fighting or watching the fights, so security in the ludus is light. There aren't many guards about.'

He jerked his head towards the door. 'Go on, then. What are you waiting for?'

'Thank you, Lanista,' said Isi.

'Thanks for everything, Crassus,' said Quin. 'We won't forget what you've done for us.'

'And we're sorry... about Hector,' added Lucius.

Crassus nodded.

He looks old, thought Lucius. *And tired. He doesn't want this job any more.*

As they raced down the corridor towards the exit, Lucius suddenly skidded to a halt.

'What is it?' cried Isi.

'Come on!' shouted Quin.

'Listen!' said Lucius. There was that faint clanking again – the sound that had kept him awake for most of the previous night. Again, he couldn't be sure where it was coming from.

'Yeah, so what?' said Quin. 'It's probably someone in the cell block, or the slave quarters.'

'No,' said Lucius. 'I was hearing it all last night – when everyone should have been asleep.'

'Come on,' said Isi. 'There'll be guards here any minute.'

Lucius pressed his fingers to his forehead, trying to concentrate. 'Think about it,' he said to them. 'Sergius must have come back here to the ludus after he left us, otherwise he wouldn't have been among the fighters today. So he would have had to hide Val somewhere close by in order to bring her food and water.'

'True,' said Quin – 'which is why we need to get out of here so we can start looking for her. There are loads of old warehouses and abandoned buildings in this part of the city where he could have imprisoned her.'

'I think she's closer than that,' said Lucius. There was something nagging at the very edges of his memory, something Sergius had once said to him.

I found myself a place to live, he'd said. *A tiny little room not far from here. I stole food from the kitchens, and I could sneak into the amphitheatre whenever I wanted without a ticket.*

'Where would you have to hide to give yourself access to the ludus kitchens and the amphitheatre?' he asked them.

Isi frowned. 'In the underground passage,' she said. 'The one they dug to connect this place with the hypogeum…'

Lucius clicked his fingers. 'Underground!' he cried. 'That's it! Sergius told me about this room he once lived in before he came here, and he said the Lupercal reminded him of it because it was underground.'

'But you can't hide someone down there,' said Isi. 'It's just a tunnel.'

'We should look, anyway,' said Quin, and the three of them ran off in the other direction towards the staircase that led to the subterranean passage.

A minute later, they were standing at the bottom of the steps, staring down the narrow, brick-walled walkway, lit by torches placed at regular intervals along both walls.

'It's just a tunnel, like I said,' said Isi despairingly.

At the far end, they could vaguely make out where it opened up into the hypogeum, the network of underground spaces beneath the arena. The clanking was still audible down here – more so than on the ground floor – yet, maddeningly, it was still not possible to work out the direction it was coming from.

They moved on down the tunnel. Lucius ran his hands over the walls, hoping to find a secret doorway hidden in the brickwork. There was nothing.

They could hear and smell the animals in the hypogeum before they caught sight of them. It brought back all sorts of unhappy memories for Lucius. In the half-light of the cavernous interior, they glimpsed shadowy figures slinking past iron-barred enclosures, and their ears rang with echoing yowls and screeches and the crashing of bodies against cage doors. Isi moved to the right of the tunnel exit, where a door was set into the outer wall of the hypogeum. Its wood was so dark it almost blended into the surrounding stonework. She tried the handle. It wouldn't open.

'Locked,' said Quin. 'Probably just some storeroom.'

'Feels as if it might be bolted from the inside,' she said.

'Impossible,' said Lucius.

'Unless…' Isi stood very still. 'Wait here,' she said, excitement building in her eyes. 'Wait right here.'

She dashed away back down the tunnel leading to the ludus.

Lucius and Quin looked at each other quizzically.

Ten minutes later, they heard a rusty bolt slide back in its groove behind the door. It creaked open, and there was Isi carrying a lighted lucerna* in her hand. In its glow they saw, just behind her, a pale, grimy-faced but ecstatic-looking Val.

* *lucerna: a Roman pottery lamp.*

Lucius nearly screamed with delight. He hugged his sister tightly, and Quin hugged them both.

'I've never been so happy to see anyone,' said Val, her voice muffled by Lucius's tunic. She sounded very frail. Her lips were cracked from thirst. 'I thought I was going to die down here. How did you find me?'

'Don't speak,' said Quin, fetching her a ladle of water from a nearby drinking trough. 'Here, drink this.'

Val glugged the water, spilling it down her tunic in her haste.

She looked up at her brothers again as if checking they were really there, and then burst into tears. 'I really, *really* thought I was going to die,' she sobbed. 'I thought the rats would eat me when I got too weak to move. You won't believe the nightmares I had. How did you find me?'

'You have Isi to thank for that,' said Lucius, glancing up at her. 'What gave you the idea that she was behind that door?'

'Maybe you've forgotten that day we sneaked into Ravilla's basement study,' she said. 'Follow me, I'll show you.'

She led them all back through the door into an extremely dark, narrow corridor. The dim, yellow gleam from the lucerna was their only light source. There was the stale, musty smell that Lucius recalled, and the feeling of claustrophobia. It instantly pulled him back to that afternoon more than three years ago when he and Isi had gone exploring down here, hoping to find out more about his uncle's shady dealings. But they had come from the other side – down a set of steps in the ludus. They'd had no idea that the corridor also gave access to the hypogeum.

A door off the corridor opened into a tiny, black cell. The door had a key in its lock. 'I found the key in Secundus's side room,' said Isi – 'just like I did last time, remember?'

'I remember,' said Lucius. Secundus had been their boss when Lucius and Isi used to work in the ludus kitchens.

'Val, you poor thing,' said Quin peering inside the room. 'You must have been scared out of your wits in this darkness.'

'It was horrible,' she sniffed. On the floor lay a rusty iron bar. Val stepped past Quin into the room and picked it up. She banged it against an old lead water pipe that ran along the wall. It made a harsh clanking sound.

'That was what I heard in my cell last night,' said Lucius. 'You kept me awake all night, Val.'

'Good!' she said with a sulky smile.

Isi pointed to the far end of the corridor. 'Ravilla's old study is down there,' she said. 'But it's not used now. In fact, it looks as though this whole basement area has been derelict since his death. We didn't realise when we sneaked down here that time, but he must have used this underground tunnel as his own personal route to the hypogeum. Ravilla was one of the bigwigs in charge of building the amphitheatre, so it makes sense that he would need regular access to it. After the main tunnel was dug, there was no more need for this one. It was abandoned and forgotten by everyone until Sergius chanced upon it.'

'Can we get out of here now,' begged Val. 'Please?!'

A few minutes later they were on the concourse outside the ludus. Val drank in great gulps of fresh air and did a little twirl of delight, letting the sun warm her bare arms. Already, small blooms of colour had begun appearing in her cheeks. She stopped at the Meta Sudans fountain to wash her face and drink some more water. Then they made their way north towards Faustina's apartment.

When they got there, they were surprised to find that Faustina had a house guest. He was about four feet tall, covered in fur and had already eaten all her figs.

'Simio!' cried Val, throwing her arms around him. 'What are you doing here?'

'He's been here for hours,' said Faustina. 'He brought a note for you, Val. I think it must be for you – anyway, he wouldn't let me take it from him.'

Val prised the papyrus note, now sticky with fig juice, from Simio's hand, and carefully unfolded it. Her eyes widened as she read it.

'Don't keep us in suspense,' said Quin. 'What does it say?'

'I can't tell you,' said Val, refolding the note and looking up at them. 'It may be good news. I hope it's good news. I have to go.'

'What?' cried Quin.

'But you've only just got here,' said Faustina. 'At least stay for something to eat.'

'No,' insisted Val. 'It's important I go right now. I'll grab a snack from a street vendor. Come on, Simio.' The chimp hopped off the table and bounded over to her side.

'Are you sure we can't come with you?' said Lucius. 'After all you've been through, do you really have to do this alone?'

'I won't be alone,' said Val, smiling at her chimp. 'Simio will protect me, won't you, Sim?' She made for the door. 'I'll see you all very soon.'

And then they were gone.

Quin and Lucius gathered at the window and watched their little sister, with Simio loping along beside her, make her way south along the Vicus Longus towards the city centre. Meanwhile, Isi helped Faustina set the table for lunch. 'I had another visitor this morning,' remarked Faustina. 'That nice young lawyer friend of yours – Gaius. He told me he's filed his lawsuit against Glabrio and the trial is set to take place as soon as the Roman Games are over – the day after tomorrow.'

CHAPTER XIV

19 SEPTEMBER

It was the day of the trial of Marcus Acilius Glabrio. The spectators' gallery of the courtroom in the Basilica Julia was packed. More benches had to be brought in to accommodate all those who had come to observe the proceedings. Hundreds more stood watching from the nave, and a crowd numbering in the thousands had gathered in the Forum outside.

By mid-morning there was nowhere left to stand. People stood in the porticoes and the temple entrances, on the balconies and rooftops. Some had even clambered up onto fountains and statues, desperate for a place near the action. Criers stood on the steps of the basilica, reporting the speeches and testimony, often word for word, for the benefit of the crowd outside.

The multitudes had gathered there, not in anticipation of a defeat for Glabrio – no one expected that – but mainly out of curiosity. They simply couldn't believe that anyone could be so foolhardy as to take on the consul. The lawyer who had brought the lawsuit might as well have signed his own death warrant. Was he really accusing Glabrio of murdering Emperor Titus? What a charge to bring against such a man! Did he not realise that, aside from the emperor himself, the consul was the most powerful man in Rome? And who was this upstart young lawyer anyway, without a single successful case to his name? Very few had heard of Gaius Horatius Canio, but all agreed that, whoever this fool was, watching him getting butchered by Glabrio's legal team would make for entertaining theatre. Now the games were over, this was easily the hottest show in town.

Among those in the spectators' gallery were Lucius, Quin and Isi, all of them in freshly created disguises, having hired Mutio's services the night before. They had arrived at the basilica early to be sure of getting good seats. As the diminutive figure of Gaius entered the courtroom, many of those on the benches around them began booing and hissing. Of course, Glabrio had packed the court with his supporters, just like last time. Gaius didn't react; he merely took a seat at a small table to one side of the praetor's podium.

The praetor entered next, accompanied by clerks

of the court. The praetor bore an ugly bruise on his forehead from its collision with Glabrio's marble floor three days earlier. His expression was stiff, possibly a little tense, as he took his seat in the curule chair on the podium. The court was now in session. The only element missing was the defendant himself, with his legal team.

As the minutes went by with no sign of Glabrio, the murmuring began among the court attendants and spectators. Would the consul even bother to show up, or would he regard the lawsuit with contempt and simply ignore it? Lucius could see Gaius attempting to appear composed, but the tautness in his shoulders betrayed his nervous state. If Glabrio didn't show, was there anything he could do? At one point he looked up and tried to catch the praetor's eye, but the praetor was preoccupied with his notes and didn't see him.

Eventually, just as the praetor was about to send a court attendant to find him, Glabrio entered the basilica, to an eruption of cheers from the benches. Flanked by twelve lictors and trailed by his advocate, Quintilius Hostilius Sejanus, and half a dozen legal aides, he strode down the central aisle of the nave and took his place in the middle of a long table near the podium, facing Gaius. The contrast between his enormous team and little Gaius all on his own was both comical and unnerving.

Glabrio appeared cheerful and relaxed, his dark eyes twinkling merrily beneath their heavy lids, his thin lips curved in a serene smile. Lucius tried to put himself in the consul's sandals. He supposed the man probably had few cares or concerns. He was due to be married in a few days, after all. His consulship was coming to an end and he'd no doubt secured himself a cushy proconsular appointment, governing a peaceful province somewhere in the sun where he and his bride could spend a pleasant year. He was fabulously wealthy and enormously powerful. What could he possibly have to complain about? There was the minor vexation of those pesky Valerii boys, who had slipped through his fingers once again, but he would surely recapture them soon. And then there was this irritating lawsuit... But the Canio boy clearly had nothing on him – he'd demonstrated that much last time, and the boo-boys on the benches would shout him down as they'd been paid to do, and Sejanus would deal with any legal arguments that needed to be made... Yes, Lucius had to concede, the self-satisfied smile did seem justified. Glabrio barely seemed to be listening as Gaius rose to his feet and began making his argument.

'Gentlemen of the court,' said Gaius, 'today it is my intention to demonstrate that on the Ides of September last year, Marcus Acilius Glabrio, Consul of Rome, murdered the late emperor Titus Flavius Caesar Vespasianus Augustus.'

This produced a ripple of astonished gasps across the benches and the nave, and then, after the criers had relayed the statement, right around the Forum outside. It wasn't that people didn't already know what the trial was about – the details of the lawsuit had been announced in the Forum that morning – it was just that most of them hadn't quite believed it until now. Glabrio did not react – his smile remained as placid as ever. But his supporters on the benches responded with anger. They booed, hissed and whistled. There were cries of 'Shame!' and 'Crucify him!' and 'Latrine lawyer!' – this last, a term for lawyers who got their business from rumours spread in public latrines.

The praetor called for quiet, but the noise scarcely diminished. Gaius had to force his voice louder to be heard, which made him sound screechy and shrill. 'I want to tell the story,' he cried, 'of an ambitious man, a frustrated man, who craved power and knew he would never achieve it while Titus ruled...' Lucius couldn't make out much more than this – until suddenly, like a stubborn little boat refusing to sink beneath the stormy sea, the lawyer's voice resurfaced: 'I have evidence,' he squeaked. 'Testimony from men of great status. From Senator Quintus Valerius Aquila, and my own father, Senator Galerius Horatius Canio. From the renowned physician Diomedes. Tragically, all these men are now deceased, cut down before their time – silenced, I would contend, by the same man who murdered the emperor, the man seated opposite me now, Marcus Acilius Glabrio. He murdered them all to prevent them from exposing his foul crime...'

By now, the din from the benches amounted to a

wall of noise, above which Gaius's voice was struggling to climb. He turned to the praetor in desperation. But the praetor's attention was on Sejanus, who had risen to his feet and was calling 'Objection!'

'Yes, what is it?' asked the praetor.

The courtroom hushed to hear Sejanus speak.

'This is all hearsay, your honour,' he said. 'He's putting words in the mouths of the dead.'

'I'm inclined to agree,' said the praetor.

Of course you are, thought Lucius, remembering the way Glabrio had forced him to grovel a few days earlier.

'Kindly confine your witnesses to the living from now on,' the praetor told Gaius.

'What about something *written* by Diomedes?' Gaius asked him.

The praetor considered this. 'That ought to be all right, so long as you can prove he wrote it.'

'I'm sure I can, your honour. But I will not show it here unless I have the court's guarantee that it will not be taken from me and destroyed, as happened last time.'

This caused a few surprised mutterings. 'Evidence from Diomedes destroyed? What is he talking about?'

Some of the boo-boys tried to heckle him, but they were hushed by their neighbours on the benches, who were becoming intrigued by what Gaius had to say.

For the first time, Lucius saw Glabrio's smile falter

slightly. His lips tightened into something closer to a grimace as Sejanus leaned towards him and began speaking rapidly into his ear. He could only imagine their conversation: *But we destroyed the autopsy report – didn't we?*

The praetor cast a nervous glance towards the consul before replying to Gaius: 'You have the court's guarantee.'

From a bag beneath his table, Gaius drew out a small, leather-covered casket. The courtroom was completely silent as he opened the casket with a key and drew out two scrolls. People leaned forward in their seats. A casket, yellowing scrolls – this was impressive. It had the look and feel of *evidence*.

'Here,' said Gaius, holding up the fatter of the two scrolls, 'is Diomedes's report of the autopsy he carried out on Emperor Titus, in which he concludes that the emperor was deliberately poisoned... And this,' he added, holding up the slimmer scroll, 'is a signed affidavit from Diomedes stating that Consul Glabrio forced him to change the autopsy report to read that Titus died of a fever.'

This provoked a huge upswelling of gasps and other astonished noises, which spread through the courtroom and out of the basilica doors to the furthermost corners of the Forum. Diomedes was a greatly respected figure. If he had believed that the emperor had been poisoned, that changed everything. Glabrio's jeerleaders shouted 'Lies!', 'Treason!',

'Behead him!', 'Feed him to the lions!' – but few heard them amid the general clamour of shocked murmurs.

Sejanus was once again on his feet. 'Objection, your honour,' he bellowed. 'He is assuming a fact not in evidence. This could have been written by anyone. He cannot prove it was written by Diomedes.'

'You will need to prove its authenticity before it can be accepted as evidence,' the praetor agreed.

'Certainly, your honour,' said Gaius. 'To do so, I will need to call my first witness.' He nodded to a clerk of the court, who hurried away. The clerk returned a few minutes later in the company of a small, elderly man – smaller even than Gaius – with a long nose and large, rather bulbous eyes.

'State your name,' Gaius said to the man, once he had taken his place before the podium.

'Gnaeus Stilio,' said the man in a firm, quiet voice that somehow carried right around the nave.

'And what is your profession?'

'I am a handwriting expert,' he said.

'I have here,' said Gaius, holding up a papyrus document, 'a sample of Diomedes's signature, which appears at the bottom of a medical prescription, kindly provided to me by his widow.' He then partly opened the scroll of the autopsy report, sufficient to reveal the signature scrawled at the bottom. 'Gnaeus Stilio,' he said. 'Please can you compare these two signatures and then tell me whether they were written by the same hand?'

Stilio leaned in close, settling his gaze first on one signature and then on the other. Eventually, he straightened, and gave a small nod. 'Yes,' he said. 'They were both written by the same hand.'

Gaius then asked him to examine the signature on the affidavit and compare it to the other two. More silent minutes went by before Stilio turned back to Gaius. 'All three,' he stated, 'are undoubtedly the work of the same person.'

Another buzz of excited whispers broke out around the courtroom.

'Objection, your honour,' cried Sejanus, bouncing to his feet. 'How do we know this man is an expert? What are his credentials? He may have been paid to say these things by the plaintiff.'

'You mean like you paid Vedrix and Mikon and Pavo?' cried a voice from the benches, causing a fresh outburst of surprised exclamations. Glabrio's heavies looked around with murder in their eyes, trying to locate the scoundrel who had dared to say such a thing. Only Lucius and Isi knew that it had been Quin.

'Order! Order in court!' shouted the praetor. 'I will not tolerate spectators yelling out slanderous statements. Whoever said that will be thrown out if he so much as opens his mouth again.' He peered down at Gaius. 'So, tell us: can this man prove he's a handwriting expert?'

Stilio looked affronted by the allegation. 'If I'm not,' he said, 'then I have to ask how it is that my services are in such high demand in this city. Almost every day I am called upon by some client or other to verify signatures on contracts, wills and other legal documents. Why, not three months ago, the consul himself had cause to call upon me. If he does not think me an expert, then I must ask why he bothered to call upon me.'

This speech prompted such a wild outbreak of laughter that the barracking by Glabrio's stooges was once again drowned out. Sejanus, frowning now, turned to Glabrio, who grimly shrugged and nodded: it was true, he had used the man. For the first time, Glabrio actually looked uncomfortable. Lucius noticed the sheen of sweat high on his forehead, and the way he fidgeted restlessly with the folds of his toga.

Before Sejanus had an opportunity to respond, there was a great commotion at the entrance to the basilica. Everyone turned to look as two heralds entered the nave and blew great blasts of their horns. 'Behold!' cried one. 'The emperor!' They advanced at the head of a dozen lictors, two abreast, all marching in perfect time, followed by six white-liveried slaves who bore on their shoulders a golden litter encrusted with jewels. Behind the litter marched a dozen more lictors.

A personal visit from the emperor? This was unheard of! Bewilderment could be read in everyone's faces. Yet no one dared speak. Silence reigned in the courtroom, but for the tramp-tramp-tramp of the lictors' marching feet. When the litter bearers reached the podium, they carefully lowered their royal cargo to the floor. A curtain was pulled aside, and out stepped Titus Flavius Caesar Domitianus Augustus – otherwise known as Domitian. He was thirty years old, tall and handsome in his imperial purple toga. His dark hair was thinning at the forehead and crown. His large eyes were dark and dour, possessing none of the sparkle and wit of his elder brother, nor the genial good nature of his father. This was not a man who appeared at ease in the company of ordinary people. In fact, no one could remember having seen him in public before – except at the games, when he was almost totally obscured by his entourage in the imperial box.

So why was he here?

That was the question on everybody's minds, if not on their lips, as Domitian and six of his most senior attendants and bodyguards took their places on the benches behind Glabrio and his team. Those who had been sitting there scrambled from their seats to make way for the imperial party. The emperor, once comfortably seated, made a waving gesture with his hand, the signal for the proceedings to continue.

During all this, Sejanus had been whispering urgently to Glabrio, who was responding with sharp, birdlike nods of his head. Now and then he would glance briefly behind him towards the emperor seated a few rows back. An oily sheen of sweat now covered most of his face.

Sejanus rose to his feet. 'Your honour,' he said gravely, 'my client concedes that the autopsy report by Diomedes is genuine. He further concedes that he instructed Diomedes to change it. But it's important to understand that in doing so, he was merely acting in the best interests of the state. Can you imagine what would have happened if it had come out at that stage that someone had murdered the emperor? Who knows what conclusions suspicious minds might have reached? We might have faced rebellions in the legions, the elevation of rival candidates for the imperium.* It could easily have been the Year of the Four Emperors** all over again. My client understood this danger. He knew that it was vitally important to protect the people from the hideous truth about how their emperor met his end. Indeed, we should thank my client for his prompt and decisive response to this crisis, and shudder to imagine what our lives might now be like had he allowed Diomedes to reveal the full, ghastly truth. We are very fortunate to bask in the benign and glorious rule of our beloved Lord and God, Domitian, whose magnificent presence now graces this chamber, and for that we have, at least in part, to thank my client, Consul Glabrio... Now, for the plaintiff to infer from these actions that my client had something to do with the death of Titus, is utterly

* imperium: the emperor's right to rule.
** Year of the Four Emperors: AD 69, when the emperors Galba, Otho and Vitellius were overthrown one after the other, and Vespasian became the first emperor of the Flavian dynasty.

fanciful and absurd, not to say deeply offensive – and unless he can come up with some convincing evidence to substantiate this allegation, we strongly advise him to withdraw it or face a lawsuit for slander.'

Sejanus sat down to silence.

The case was turning into one of the most dramatic events anyone could remember. Had Glabrio really just admitted that Titus had been murdered, and that he had deliberately altered the autopsy report? And had he really just admitted to all of this in front of Titus's brother, the present emperor?

No one knew how to react, least of all Glabrio's supporters, who were starting to look a little fearful that their patron might not be around for much longer. The only smile in the courtroom was affixed to the face of Glabrio. He patted Sejanus on the back to congratulate him on his speech, which he appeared to believe had won the day. Sejanus didn't respond. His usually ruddy complexion had turned ashen.

Gaius took the floor. 'Your honour, my learned colleague demands convincing evidence that Consul Glabrio murdered the late emperor. I shall now give him that evidence. I call my second witness.'

The smile froze on Glabrio's face when he saw who this witness was. He mopped his gleaming face with the sleeve of his toga as he stared disbelievingly at her. The little old slave woman, Aleta, was supported by Valeria, who held her by the arm as they came through a side door and approached the podium.

Sejanus whispered desperately in Glabrio's ear, no doubt demanding to know who this person was. But Glabrio wouldn't, or couldn't, reply.

Lucius wasn't surprised to see Aleta and Val appear, and neither were Quin and Isi – indeed, they had all been looking forward to this moment. The note Valeria had received via Simio had been from Aleta, requesting an urgent meeting. At the meeting, she'd told Val that she'd decided to testify. Then the seven of them – Lucius, Quin, Isi, Faustina, Valeria, Gaius and Aleta – had all met at Gaius's favourite popina, near the Forum, and had planned this as the climax of the show.

'Thank you for coming here today,' Gaius said to Aleta once she was standing before him in the courtroom. 'I know how difficult this was for you. You are a very brave lady.'

Aleta nodded. She was clearly scared, refusing to look anywhere but at Gaius. He asked her to state her name and her job, which she did. Then he asked her to tell him where she had been and what she had seen on the Ides of September the previous year.

'I was at the emperor's villa,' she said. 'I came as part of the master's retinue during his stay there. I was in the courtyard behind the kitchen, throwing out some vegetable peelings. Breakfast had been served and cleared. The slaves had all gone back to their quarters except for me. The kitchen was empty apart from Bibulus the cook, who was seated at the table surrounded by recipes, making plans for lunch. He had some sea-hare fresh-caught, and he was trying to decide on what dishes he should serve with it. Then the master came into the kitchen and began talking to Bibulus. He thought Bibulus was alone. Neither of them saw me in the courtyard. I crept closer to the kitchen door. I hid in the shadows there, and I saw the master hand a very small bottle to Bibulus. He told Bibulus to pour its contents into the emperor's meal. I remember being very scared when I heard this. I was scared that if I made a noise and the master found me there, he'd kill me. I was so scared of making a noise, I wouldn't even put my bucket down on the floor. Bibulus was scared, too. Even so, he refused. The master threatened to kill his wife and his three children. So Bibulus nodded and took the bottle, and the master left. That's what I saw.'

Lucius watched Glabrio with interest as Aleta gave her testimony. He saw the flaring of anger in his eyes, and the fearful trembling that afflicted his arms and shoulders, and the pulsing vein in his forehead. No longer comfortable in his seat, the consul squirmed restlessly, fists clenching and unclenching. He seemed to want to tear this woman limb from limb. The fact that he couldn't was pure torture for him. Lucius thought about all the suffering this man had inflicted on him and his family this past year, and it gave him a quiet thrill of pleasure to see Glabrio finally taste the consequences of his vile actions.

Sejanus was on his feet almost before Aleta had finished speaking. Addressing the entire courtroom, he furiously declared: 'And who will take the word of a slave against that of a citizen, a consul even?'

In response there was a shuffling movement on the benches behind him and a figure rose to his feet. It took people a moment to realise that it was the emperor.

'I do,' said Domitian in a deep, slightly brittle voice. 'Aleta is well known to me. She was bought by my father originally, from the slave markets of the east. I now regret that she was ever sold to Glabrio. Aleta helped bring me up. From her I learned many things, but the most important of these was honesty. Her very name is Greek for "truth-teller".'

That short speech by the emperor marked the end of the trial, as Sejanus immediately conceded defeat. It also marked the end for Marcus Acilius Glabrio. A criminal trial inevitably followed a few weeks later. In the course of this, Glabrio's many other crimes, including the murders of Aquila, Canio and Diomedes, came to light, as previously intimidated witnesses queued up to give their testimony. Glabrio, by now a frightened, diminished figure, was forced to sit and listen as witness after witness spoke of the suffering he had inflicted on them during his reign of terror.

Gaius Canio, whose fame as a lawyer had skyrocketed following his performance in the civil action against Glabrio, was invited to join the prosecution team for the criminal trial. He accepted, but insisted, out of respect for his friends Quintus, Lucius and Valeria, that their mother Caecilia's role in Glabrio's crimes should never be disclosed, and that her name should not even be mentioned in court. His colleagues acceded to this demand. Even so, Caecilia never recovered from the shock of her fiancé's fall. Glabrio was found guilty and sentenced to death. He was beheaded on the Kalends* of November. The following day, Caecilia's body was found in her bedroom beside an empty bottle of hemlock. She left no message.

Her death came as a shock to her children – for even after everything, she was still the woman who had given birth to them. But this dark event marked the close of a dark chapter in their lives, and the beginning of a new and infinitely happier phase. Lucius, Quin and Valeria moved back to their family villa on the Esquiline Hill. Their father's bust was restored to the atrium and the little wooden dog that had been Aquila's favourite among the household gods, and which Lucius had kept with him during all his adventures, was restored to the family shrine. Lucius was overjoyed to be reunited with his real-life dog, Argos, and the two of them became, once again,

* *Kalends: the first of the month.*

inseparable companions. Whether Lucius was in the library, in the grounds, or on one of his long walks in the hills and forests east of the city, Argos was always by his side.

Isidora moved in with Faustina, although she was a frequent visitor to the villa. She liked to tease Lucius that her only reason for visiting was to check up on her tiger, Kato, who had his own enclosure in the grounds. But she would always seek Lucius out in the library after she'd seen Kato and they would spend long afternoons together. Sometimes he'd read her some poetry, or, if the weather was warm, they might head down to the Piscina Publica* for a swim. Neither of them liked to think or talk too much about the recent past. They would in time, but for now it was all a bit too raw. The only event from that time that Lucius liked to recall was the day they'd spent together on Lake Albano.

The following summer, a year after that first visit, he and Isi returned to Gaius's villa on the lake, along with Quin, Val, Simio and Argos. They enjoyed a splendid few weeks there, fishing, swimming, eating and playing. One afternoon, they had a picnic on a grassy bank next to the lake. Gaius's luxury barge, with its polished cedarwood hull and gold fittings, lay at anchor a hundred paces from the shore, bobbing in the placid blue water. After they had eaten, Quin, Gaius and Val tossed a ball between them while Simio

* *Piscina Publica: public swimming pool.*

tried to snatch it from them, and Argos barked at the ducks. Lucius and Isi lay side by side on the grass and he told her that the memory of the day they'd spent here the previous summer had kept him going through the bleakest times – 'especially,' he said, 'the kiss.'

'You mean like this?' said Isi, edging closer and kissing him on the lips.

'Exactly like that,' said Lucius dizzily. He stared at her, failing as ever to interpret her smile.

'I don't suppose you'd ever want to get married,' he said.

When she didn't reply, he turned away. 'Stupid idea,' he muttered. 'Why would you want to marry someone like me?'

He heard her dark, mischievous giggle. 'Hm, let me think. Handsome, brave, clever… No, I can't think of a single reason why I'd possibly want to marry you.'

He spun round to face her, his mouth open. 'You forgot *rich*,' he laughed. 'And *patrician*. Did you know you can trace our family right back to the early Republic?'

Isi's smile faded. 'None of that impresses me, Lu. You should know that by now. If you think that's what's important, you should go off and marry a patrician girl.'

His face fell. 'Isi, at some point I've got to grow up, embark on the cursus honorum,* like all men of my

---

* *cursus honorum: the political career that was considered proper for a Roman citizen of senatorial rank.*

rank. I know for a fact that Quin won't do it, so it's bound to fall to me. I'll be a tribune, then a senator. I'd sort of hoped that you'd be there by my side.'

Isi was quiet for a time, staring at the clouds. Eventually, she said: 'I don't know if any of that's me. Maybe I'll change, I don't know. We're still so young. We don't have to decide anything now, do we?' She bit her lip and turned to him and he saw an unmistakable teardrop in her eye. He felt his heart closing down like a flower being crushed in a fist.

'You don't want to marry me,' he said. 'Just say it.'

'I don't know,' she replied, sadly, her finger slowly tracing the scar on his chest. 'You remember that time when we first met and I asked you what you were? Well, now I know what you are, aristo-boy. What I'm still trying to figure out is who *I* am. I mean, I find it hard to imagine myself as the wife of a senator... On the other hand, I'm not sure I can stand the thought of you marrying anyone else.'

He kissed her, and they remained like that, in each other's arms, for a long time. Lucius felt the warmth of the sun on his shoulders and, more intensely than ever, the soft, amber-scented presence of the girl he loved. He held on to her fiercely, almost angrily, as if daring fate to even try and pull them apart.

At some point – it might have been hours or minutes later – she broke away from him. 'My mind,' she whispered, 'is in a complete mess, and for that I totally blame you, Lucius Valerius.'

Then she got to her feet. 'Race you to the boat!' she smiled, and they both sprinted across the grass and dived into the sparkling blue water.

EPILOGUE

WHAT HAPPENED TO THEM?

I had intended to give you a summary here of how the lives of our four main characters panned out. But when I came to write it, I realised that I didn't really know, and even if I did, perhaps it wasn't my place to say. So I've decided instead to tell you what I *think* happened to them and leave it up to you whether to believe me or not.

Valeria, I suspect, turned out the happiest of all of them. She grew up to be an eccentric young lady, to say the least, with her devotion to a certain chimpanzee, and animals in general. In fact, the Valerii villa on the Esquiline Hill became quite well known for its menagerie, as the chimp, the tiger and the elephant were joined, in time, by an injured bear, a couple of hyenas and a giraffe, which Valeria managed to rescue from the vivarium. I would love to tell you that she went on to become a respected zoologist or veterinarian, but alas, such jobs were not available to young ladies in those days. In the end, I'm afraid she did the conventional thing and became a wife. Fortunately, her sweet, sensitive, loyal and fun-loving nature found its perfect complement in the man she married, and they were very happy together. Like all Roman aristocratic wives, she spun wool in her spare time, she entertained guests and clients, she managed her estates, and she had children – three girls. And Simio, by then quite an elderly chimp, turned out to be very adept at keeping the babes entertained – though he was known occasionally to steal their bowls of fig purée.

I would love to be able to say that Quin's story ends equally happily. The truth is, no one knows. His fate, like his life, remains shrouded in myth. Quin's untamable spirit and restless need for adventure led him, perhaps inevitably, back to the legions. Under his own name this time, he rejoined the Twentieth, serving under General Agricola in Caledonia. The Phoenix of Pompeii's luck finally ran out two years later, during the Battle of Mons Graupius. He was killed during an assault on an enemy encampment – or so the official story goes. But according to the legend, a wounded Quin escaped the battle and was nursed back to health by a beautiful Caledonian princess by the name of Floree, and they escaped to Caledonia's Western Isles to live happily ever after. I know which version I prefer to believe.

But what of Lucius and Isi? I can guess what you're wondering: Did they ever get married? The answer is, I'm not sure – but I think probably not. Although they loved each other dearly, Isi was never really cut out to be a dutiful wife. The good news is that they remained close friends throughout their lives. Lucius became a well-respected senator who, like his father, devoted himself to helping the poor and underprivileged of Rome. He avoided all visits to the Flavian Amphitheatre, though he did occasionally drop by at the Ludus Romanus to say hello to his old boss, Crassus. Lucius married a delightful young patrician lady, whose father boasted that he could trace his family all the way back to King Romulus. They had three children, all boys. The eldest of them, Quintus, would in time inherit the family villa on the Esquiline – assuming Lucius could persuade him not to become a gladiator. As for Isi, she never married, preferring the freedom that came with spinsterhood. She went into business with Faustina, making and selling jewellery and religious ornaments. During the reign of Domitian, the cult of the Egyptian goddess Isis became very popular, and Isi and Faustina did very well for themselves selling Isis rings, pendants and figurines. As Isi often used to say, her Egyptian heritage came in handy after all!

FRIENDS AND

Aquila

Quintus Valerius Aquila was the father of Lucius, Quin and Valeria. A distinguished Roman senator, he loved reading and disliked the gladiatorial games with their violence and bloodshed. Wrongly accused of treason, Aquila was forced to flee from Rome, abandoning his family. Only his younger son, Lucius, believed in his innocence and was determined to prove it.

Caecilia

Aquila's wife is Caecilia Valeria Aquilae, a dutiful wife and mother who enjoys her comfortable life as a respectable Roman matron. She is distraught when Aquila disappears and she has to move her family into a shabby flat in a run-down suburb of Rome. Like most people, she believes that Aquila is guilty of treason.

RELATIONS

Isidora
The Egyptian slave Isidora first
meets Lucius when they find
themselves working together
at the Ludus Romanus, the
gladiator school owned by
Lucius's uncle, Gaius Valerius
Ravilla. Set free after the death
of her master, she becomes a
freelance gladiator travelling
around the Mediterranean. But,
fiercely independent though she
is, her story becomes inextricably
interwoven with that of Lucius
and his fight for justice.

Valeria
Valeria Prima Aquila, the youngest
member of the family, is only a
child when the series begins, but
has to grow up quickly. She is
patient, intelligent and especially
clever with animals. Simio, a chimp
who has escaped from the arena,
becomes her trusty sidekick.

A selected list of Scribo titles

The prices shown below are correct at the time of going to press. However, The Salariya Book Company reserves the right to show new retail prices on covers, which may differ from those previously advertised.

Gladiator School by Dan Scott

1	Blood Oath	978-1-908177-48-3	£6.99
2	Blood & Fire	978-1-908973-60-3	£6.99
3	Blood & Sand	978-1-909645-16-5	£6.99
4	Blood Vengeance	978-1-909645-62-2	£6.99
5	Blood & Thunder	978-1-910184-20-2	£6.99
6	Blood Justice	978-1-910184-43-1	£6.99

Iron Sky by Alex Woolf

1	Dread Eagle	978-1-909645-00-4	£9.99

Aldo Moon by Alex Woolf

1	Aldo Moon and the Ghost at Gravewood Hall		
		978-1-908177-84-1	£6.99

Chronosphere by Alex Woolf

1	Time out of Time	978-1-907184-55-0	£6.99
2	Malfunction	978-1-907184-56-7	£6.99
3	Ex Tempora	978-1-908177-87-2	£6.99

Visit our website at:

www.salariya.com

All Scribo and Salariya Book Company titles can be ordered from your local bookshop, or by post from:

The Salariya Book Co. Ltd,
25 Marlborough Place
Brighton BN1 1UB

Postage and packing **free** in the United Kingdom